What Sam Knew

A Patricia Fisher Village Mystery

Book 1

Steve Higgs

Dedication

This book is dedicated to Erin Hayes. Thank you for reading Erin.

Table of Contents

Vergers are Crazy

I flinched as a shower of plaster rained down on my head. That the hammer he threw missed me was pure luck; I caught only the barest sense of it as it flew across the room and had to imagine it would have knocked me unconscious had it connected with my skull as intended.

With a squeal of fright, I darted back toward the front door.

An enraged shout followed me, 'Fisher! You interfering old busybody.'

I thought the old part of his insult was a little harsh but now wasn't the time to start a debate. He was chasing me back out of his house and I didn't want to think what might happen if he caught up to me while I was still inside.

His name was Derek Quince. For the last three weeks on and off, I had been working on a case of poison pen letters which someone in the village was sending. There was no other crime associated with it which was why it kept slipping down the priority list and had taken me three weeks to solve. Derek was writing all manner of terrible gossip and filth in his letters, carefully cutting out individual letters from magazines and newspapers to then glue them to a nondescript piece of A4 paper which he mailed from fifty miles away in Surrey. He had carefully thought out every element of the crime, covering his tracks very well and leaving no easy clues for me to latch onto.

As I used the hallway wall to ricochet off and run for the front door, I heard something smash into the wall right behind me. He was still finding things to throw and only needed to find his target once.

After three weeks, I caught him by a process of elimination. He sent seven letters in total, each to a different person, and in each of them he threatened death or serious injury and revealed what the recipient's

1

partner had been up to. Some of what he wrote turned out to be true such as Mrs Curzon cheating on her husband with his brothers. Yes, brothers. Plural. A lot of it was total guff though, invented hateful lies which I had to sift through.

My guess was that the perpetrator had to benefit in some way, so I started to look at who that might be, expanding my search outward from the letter recipients. I ignored the first letter and the most recent, believing that, if this was about achieving a particular aim, then potentially all but one of the letters were red herrings intended to disguise the true purpose of the crime.

Like I said - he covered his tracks well.

I was almost at the front door, but now I could see his mum had put the safety chain back on it after she let me in, the precautionary muscle memory of an octogenarian. It defeated me before I got to it, he was less than four metres behind me, so I would not have time to get the chain off and open the door before he slammed into me. Making a fast decision, I snagged the door frame on my left and swung into the dining room. This house was the same as every other one in the street. They were all built in the 1890s with a central hallway leading to a bathroom and kitchen at the back and the stairs to go up. To each side as you looked at it were a dining room and a living room. The living room stretched all the way to the back of the house, but the dining room only went part way where it then met the kitchen. There I could access the back door and hope to escape to where someone would hear my screams.

Derek was the verger at the village church and felt he had been overlooked when the senior verger, Harold Lilly, retired a few months ago. Mrs Fothergill on the parish council decided the appointments and had gone with the younger man, David Fothergill, her son, to take the position.

2

I honestly couldn't understand what anyone was getting excited about; it wasn't even a paid job. The vergers performed minor tasks during services and made sure the church was kept in a good state of repair. The grounds, the artefacts etcetera, all fell to the vergers to manage. But the senior verger got to hold the bible for the vicar to read from on a Sunday. I'm sure there were other, more exciting, elements to the job, but none of them should have led Derek to accuse Mrs Fothergill of laying with animals or her son of wearing leather and rubber sex wear beneath his cassock each week. He was quite descriptive in his letters, especially the one which went to the vicar and caused him to ask both Mrs Fothergill and her son, David Fothergill, to step down from the positions they so clearly coveted.

I caught Derek because he was too confident. He rejoiced that they lost, and he won, and he smiled all the way through Sunday morning service yesterday as he held the bible for the first time. I played a hunch and knocked on his door this morning intending to ask a few careful questions. His mum let me in, and here I am trying to escape with my skull intact.

'Is everything alright, dear?' asked old Enid Quince. She was sitting at the dining table with a cup of tea and a copy of the parish magazine, looking up in surprise as I hurtled through her dining room, followed sharply thereafter by her son who was suggesting some most unchristian-like things would happen when he caught me.

I hit the kitchen door with my left shoulder, bruising it almost certainly, but not caring one jot in my haste to get away. The back door was right ahead of me, the family cat sitting by it as it waited to be let out. Its eyes went wide as it saw me running like a mad woman in its direction, and like cats do, it started running. Its paws found no traction on the linoleum floor for a second so it didn't get out of the way as I expected and I

3

tripped over it, managing to snag the door handle with an outstretched hand so the back door opened as I fell into it.

I tumbled out and down a stone step to the garden path, rolling as I went. It was a painful experience, but one which I would have to reflect on later because there was no time now. Coming to rest on my back, I could see Derek coming out of the back door less than a stride behind me. His lips were pulled back in an angry grimace as he dove to land on me.

He stopped in mid-air, his body floating a yard above mine.

'Are you alright, madam?' asked Jermaine.

My ever-faithful butler had been deployed to the back garden in case Derek tried to escape, not that we needed to catch him. If I could prove he was guilty, the police would take it from there. However, for completeness, I wanted to hand the local detective, Detective Sergeant Mike Atwell, a closed case and a subdued perpetrator.

Jermaine is twenty-eight years old, stands six feet four inches tall, and is part ninja, part bodyguard and all butler. His quiet, refined, dignified manner is by choice, as is his accent, since he grew up in Jamaica. Far from sounding Caribbean, he learned to speak with an English accent by watching Downton Abbey. I have caught him brushing up by watching old episodes more than once though he thinks I don't know he owns the full set on DVD. How he came to be my butler is a rather long story, but I will tell you that I love him very dearly and could not imagine life without him around. We met on board a cruise ship where he used to work until he was offered a better position at my enormous manor house in Kent.

Derek now dangled from his hands as he caught him mid-dive as if he were a rugby ball. Changing grip, Jermaine allez-ooped Derek onto his feet right by the back door.

'Can I expect you to behave, sir?' Jermaine asked.

In reply to his question, Derek made a break for the door, trying to get back inside his house as if that would change the outcome. Jermaine reached out to snag his collar and yank him off balance. As Derek tumbled to the grass, Jermaine reached down to help me up.

'I fear you may have scuffed your coat, madam,' he said, peering at my left shoulder. 'I shall do my best to repair that when we get home.'

'You are too kind, Jermaine.' I was back on my feet, but a little out of breath, the race through the Quince house, combined with adrenaline from potential death, quite enough to spike my heart rate.

'DS Atwell advised that he would not be long, madam. Five minutes he estimated. I took the precaution of calling him when I heard your first shout. You are not hurt?'

'No, Jermaine. It was nothing more than a little additional exercise this time.' To clarify, while all I had to do this time was run away, in the past, some of my cases have been a little more... adventurous, shall we say.

My name is Patricia Fisher. I would like to be able to say that I am nobody, but I have been forced to accept that is no longer true. I live near West Malling, a delightful village in the southeast corner of England where I grew up. Until a short while ago, I had barely ever left, then a chance event led to the discovery of my husband's infidelity and that in turn resulted in a three month around the world cruise. That is where I met Jermaine, among others, and discovered my ability to unpick mysteries. Something about the way my brain is wired allows me to see through the fog of clues to find the truth beneath and that is why I now own a detective agency.

One or two of the mysteries I solved during my cruise made international headlines, which, in turn, gave me some kind of quasi-celebrity status. They also attracted the attention of the world's third richest person, the Maharaja of Zangrabar. I saved his life in a roundabout way and he gave me a house he no longer wanted. A house so big and so grand one could probably see it from space. It came with staff and it was all paid for in perpetuity.

My life might not be a perfect fairy-tale, but the bits I am possibly not happy about are eclipsed by all the things I need to feel grateful for.

'Would you like a cup of tea, dears?' asked Enid, appearing at the door with the cat curling around her feet.

From the grass, where he lay winded and trying to decide his next move, Derek squinted up at his elderly mother. 'What? You're offering them tea?'

'Of course, dear,' she replied, tutting as she looked down at her dishevelled son. 'I told you those letters would get you into trouble.'

A Fresh Case

Two hours later, I was sitting in what I thought might become my favourite room in the house (there are seventy-three rooms) as I sifted emails. I have an office a few miles away in Rochester High Street, but I have no need to go there unless I want somewhere business-like to conduct a client meeting.

The room I was in overlooked the plush gardens to the rear of the house. From my chair I could see rabbits at play under the oak trees a hundred yards away and all manner of native birds fluttering back and forth in their search for food. Squirrels too were regular visitors, though they were unhappy with my dog. Anna is a miniature Dachshund I picked up in Japan during my cruise. I had never owned a dog before and until she became mine through dint of rescuing her from Japanese mafia, I had never considered doing so. Now, like Jermaine, I couldn't imagine being without her. The vet estimated her age at four or possibly five but advised that Dachshunds often live into their twenties and fifteen would be a reasonable expectation.

Just as I thought about her, a tiny reddish-brown streak shot across the garden, barking all the way in her excitement as she tried to get to the squirrel she could see. The squirrel ran back up into the tree and threw an acorn at her. A minute later, it came down a different tree and carried on with what it was doing as Anna continued to bark at the tree she had seen it run up.

Somewhere in the house, most likely in the pantry, were her puppies. A chance encounter with the Queen's Corgis during the Maharaja of Zangrabar's coronation resulted in four perfect Dachshund Corgi cross puppies. They looked like Dachshunds to me, no different in shape or features to Anna save for their fur which was a little more coarse than hers.

7

'Tea, madam,' announced Jermaine as he came into the room with a silver tray.

I realised at that point I had been staring aimlessly out of the window at my new garden for the last ten minutes. Long enough, in fact, for my laptop to time out so the screen was blank and needed to be nudged back into life.

I turned his way with a smile as I said, 'Yes, thank you, Jermaine.' He placed the tray on the table next to me, expertly pouring tea into a china cup before setting it to my right.

He looked like he was about to ask me something when my phone began to ring. As was his practice, he answered it for me. 'Good morning. Patricia Fisher Investigation Bureau. How may I direct your call?'

I continued to scrutinise my emails, trying hard to not listen to the faint voice at the other end of the call, but hearing most of what the woman had to say anyway. After a few moments, Jermaine said, 'I have a Mrs Foy on the line, madam. She believes her husband was murdered and would like you to prove it for her.'

'Can you put her on speaker, please?'

Jermaine placed my phone on the desk and pressed the button to connect the caller to the speaker. 'Mrs Foy, you are now on speaker with Mrs Fisher.'

I spoke next. 'Mrs Foy, good morning. I'm terribly sorry for your loss. Was it recent?'

Mrs Foy sniffed deeply before answering, her grief very present. 'It was eight days ago. He fell while climbing last Sunday. The police kept his body until yesterday because I claimed it had to be murder, but they recorded a

8

verdict of death by misadventure. They've got it wrong,' she wailed, unable to keep her emotions in check.

Standing so he loomed over me, Jermaine was hurriedly making notes on a tablet, the fingers of his right hand little more than a blur.

Pressing on despite her tears, I asked, 'Why do you say that? What makes you so sure?'

'He was always such a safe climber. His quickdraw failed, that's what they said. It snapped and he fell, but he would always have at least one other safety device in place if he was climbing alone and he hasn't climbed alone in years. Plus, his quickdraws were all new. He was meticulous about keeping his equipment in good order. They said they found his fingerprints and DNA on it and were quite content his death was nothing more than a terrible accident.' She sniffed again, making that shuddering noise one gets after a prolonged bout of crying. 'He was killed, Mrs Fisher. I don't know why or who it might have been, but someone was at the climb with him last Sunday and they murdered him.'

When she fell silent, I gave myself a second to think. In the month since I opened the business, I have had a lot of enquiries for my detective services. None of it was very exciting though. It was a lot of cheating partners people wanted me to catch in the act; I turned down every one of those because it was just too sleazy to be associated with. I also got requests to find missing cats, stolen heirlooms which had simply been misplaced, several robberies, which were a bit more like it, Derek's silly poison pen letter nonsense, and one case of fraud. This was the first really good case and I couldn't have been more excited.

I would need to solve it before I could celebrate though.

One thing I definitely needed was more detail. 'Mrs Foy, I need to conduct a preliminary investigation before I take the case and would like to visit you as soon as it is convenient. Are you free now?'

'Oh, um,' she sniffed. 'I'm a bit of a mess. They just released his body, you see. I need to arrange his funeral now. Susie, that's my daughter, she's helping of course, but there's so much to do suddenly. When do you want to come?'

'As soon as it is convenient, Mrs Foy,' I repeated.

'Yes. Yes, you said that, didn't you? I suppose now is as good of a time as any.' Mrs Foy gave me her address and promised to make herself presentable by the time we got there. I assured her it was not necessary, but I understood that she didn't want to meet people while looking at her absolute worst.

Once disconnected, I waited for Jermaine to finish making his notes, but he had already performed that task and moved on to another. He turned the tablet so I could see it. 'This is a quickdraw, madam. I believed it might help to give context to the investigation.' On the screen was a device that looked like two carabiners with a piece of material joining them. I had no idea what its purpose might be but at least now I could picture what it was supposed to look like. 'Shall I start the car?' he asked.

That Jermaine asked about *the* car, was a clear indication that I had a favourite. Arriving at the manor house a month ago, I discovered a garage full of cars located at the far end of the west wing. That the house has a west wing is a clear indication of its size. In it were fifteen cars, ranging from a Mini Cooper to a tricked-out Range Rover. There was a Rolls Royce just in case I fancied afternoon tea at the Ritz in London and wanted to arrive in style, and no less than three Ferraris. I added another car to the collection, the one I was driving at the time. It wasn't mine. I sort of lucked into it after my battered old Ford Fiesta caught fire and exploded. It was a 1954 Aston Martin DB2/4 Drophead Coupé in silver with a tan leather interior. It had been converted into a ragtop by Bertone directly after manufacture at the owner's request and was the single most elegant and beautiful car I had ever seen. It was on lease from a local Aston Martin dealer when I got my hands on it, but I did a deal with them and it was mine now.

As Jermaine went to warm the engine, I packed a few things into my handbag and called a friend.

A Man on the Inside

Detective Sergeant Mike Atwell was my kind of person. He understood the rules but wasn't necessarily going to follow them if they didn't make sense for a particular set of circumstances. We bonded over a case when I first returned to England and now he was my man on the inside. The inside of the police, that is, and the one who I could get answers from most of the time.

'Patricia,' he answered his phone. 'What can I do for you this morning?'

'Good morning, Mike. I have a question.'

'I expected as much. Fire away.' Mike Atwell had been a police officer for more than three decades, rising to the rank of detective sergeant more than fifteen years ago where he seemed quite content to stay. His patch covered a wide area of rural Kent where there was a lot of territory but not many people. I got the impression he was a little bored with it all. His most heinous crime in a typical week might be something like squirrel poaching in the local park, homeless people trapping them to cook. It was, in fact, legal to do so provided one caught only the grey squirrels which are listed as vermin and not the smaller, cuter red squirrels, but the park wardens went nuts about it anyway.

Mike and I had an easy relationship, where he fed me information provided it wasn't going to compromise a live case, and I took him for lunch at one of the many fine local restaurants.

'There was a death recently. A climber who fell at Great Capwood park.'

'Edward Foy?' That made things easier; he already knew the case. 'Has the widow engaged your services?'

'Yes. Just this morning. She is convinced still that it was murder so I will be investigating. What can you tell me?'

'Hmmm,' he murmured slowly. 'I doubt I can tell you anything until...'

'Until I furnish you with fish and chips,' I finished his sentence with a laugh.

He laughed too. 'I don't know anything about the case, in truth. But I can find out. Do you want to meet later? I can come by the house.' It was already lunchtime and I was off to meet Mrs Foy as soon as I was done with this call.

'How about afternoon tea? The tearoom in West Malling always serves a nice spread. Can you make four o'clock.'

'Tea at four o'clock. How very British, Patricia. I shall see you there.' With the call ended, I put my phone away, checked my makeup in the big mirror in the grand lobby and left the house.

Jermaine was already outside with the car. 'Shall I accompany you, madam?' he asked.

'Ha! So good of you to ask, Jermaine. You usually follow me when I leave you behind anyway.'

'Madam has a penchant for attracting trouble,' he replied calmly.

I couldn't argue. There were a number of incidents in the last four months when I survived only because of his reflexes. I didn't think a visit to Mrs Foy's house was likely to place me in any danger but if I left him behind, he would just fret or start polishing the silver again.

I rolled my eyes at his comment, feeling that I had to at least look wounded. 'Alright, you can come. Is it really necessary to dress like John Steed?'

Ransom Note

The next call came as I pulled away. You might think that I would have Bluetooth installed because it would add practicality to the car, but it would also ruin the sixty-five-year-old aesthetics. So, yet again, it was Jermaine who answered my phone.

'Patricia Fisher Investigation Bureau, you are through to Jermaine. How may we help this morning?'

'H-hello?' The voice was that of a woman. I placed her age at late twenties or into her thirties and local by her accent. She was unlikely to come from one of the local cities such as Maidstone as she enunciated her letters quite clearly as one ought, so wherever she now lived, she would hail from one of the villages. She wasn't confident though, her timid opener suggesting to me that she wasn't certain about calling us and might hang up at any second.

'Good morning, he repeated, trying to keep her on the line. 'This is Jermaine Clarke, Mrs Fisher's butler. I have you on speaker phone. How may we assist you?'

'This is Patricia,' I chipped in, leaning my head to the centre of the car and thus closer to the phone unnecessarily since I knew it could pick my voice up adequately wherever I sat. Giving her my first name might make us sound more friendly, I hoped. When I got nothing in response, I asked, 'Can you tell us your name? Or what it is that you are calling about. We are completely confidential.'

She said, 'Um,' and then fell silent again for a few seconds. 'Someone has taken my dog. I have a ransom note,' she finally explained the reason for her call.

I guess it is a dog owner thing because I was instantly incensed. Someone had taken her dog and was demanding money for its return. I was going to hound (no pun intended) them to the ends of the earth if I had to. 'That sounds like a case I should take, Mrs...'

'Emma. It's Miss Emma Maynard,' she provided her name to my prompt, sounding more confident now that she had explained why she was calling and already had my interest. 'Will you be taking the case then?' she asked. 'Only, I spoke with the police and they weren't much help.'

I understood why. They would be sympathetic, but their resources were stretched. Still, I would be surprised if they hadn't opened a case file and were at least looking into it. Crimes such as this usually went in spates; a gang finding a way to make easy money.

'What sort of dog is it?' I asked.

'A teacup Yorkshire Terrier. The really small ones. He only weighs three pounds. Someone could put him in their handbag and walk away.' I heard her voice catch in her throat; she was my second tearful woman in the last hour, and it said a lot about my life that I felt more empathy for the one with the missing dog than Mrs Foy with the dead husband. My own husband had chosen to cheat on me, his infidelity acting as the catalyst for the changes to my life that landed me my millionaire lifestyle.

'How long ago was the dog taken, please, and how long after that did the ransom note arrive?' Now that I was asking questions, more questions were forming in my head. Thankfully, Jermaine was at hand to takes notes again, his fingers poised for her replies.

'It happened on Saturday.'

'Two days ago?' I clarified.

16

'Yes, sorry. Yes, two days ago. He was in the garden, but when I called him in, he didn't come. I thought he had just escaped but an hour later a picture of him came through to my phone with a message. I pay them ten thousand or they send him back to me in pieces.' Her voice broke again as she relayed the content of the message.

I expected the answer of my next question to be obvious, but I asked it anyway. 'You didn't recognise the number they contacted you on?'

'It came up as withheld. I would have called them back otherwise. The police said I should let them know if I get any more messages. The first one said they would contact me with instructions, but that was two days ago, and I haven't heard from then since.'

It wasn't much to go on, that was for sure. I twitched my nose as I thought about it. Having no perceivable starting point was no reason not to take the case. I would work it out as I went along, same as always. 'Okay, Emma. I can take this case if that is what you want.' At the other end she started praising God. I talked over her, 'I will need to come to your house later today, will you be there?'

'Yes, I work from home.'

'Very good. I have your number. I will be back in touch as soon as I can but...' I glanced quickly at the clock, 'I expect to be with you around two o'clock.' I went on to outline my fees, get her address, which Jermaine wrote down, and then do my best to reassure her.

A missing dog was hardly a high-profile case, but I could manage this and the murder/death by misadventure at the same time and probably more besides. I felt a pull to take multiple cases, but in truth I didn't need to work at all, I had money in the bank and all my bills were taken care of for the rest of my life by the Maharaja. I kept going with my idea of being

17

a private investigator, because what would I do with myself if I had no job?

Little did I know how busy and crazy my life was going to get over the next few weeks.

Edward Foy

Sarah and Edward Foy lived in Allington. Once a rural community, it had been when I was little, it was now part of the urban sprawl stretching out from Maidstone town centre. It nestled the river Medway on one flank and bordered the M20 motorway on another, those physical barriers demarking it from other small villages which would otherwise all link together.

Their house was a pretty semidetached place that looked to be no more than ten years old. I wasn't a fan of the style, finding the rooms too small and the walls too thin, but now that I lived in a manor house I hadn't even paid for, I could never voice such a view.

Mrs Foy saw us coming, the curtain twitching as she reset it when we pulled up. Jermaine was swift to exit, hooking his umbrella over his left elbow and donning his bowler hat as he raced, in an ever so calm and dignified manner, to my side of the car to open my door. Today he wore a very dark grey pinstripe suit, with black brogues, plus a white shirt and a light pink tie which matched perfectly the shade of the pinstripes. He had worn his John Steed outfit on several previous occasions, the television action hero being someone Jermaine felt to be the epitome of debonair cool suaveness. He admitted as much when I quizzed him about it the first time he wore it. I don't know many homosexual men, so cannot tell if his behaviour is typical or not, but my butler can be quite flamboyant when he wants to be.

The door opened before we could reach it, Mrs Foy looking tired and a little beaten; her eyes puffy from crying and bereft of makeup as if she just didn't think it was worth bothering with if more tears were to come. She was in her late thirties as I had imagined she would be and was quite average in her appearance. She was average height at about five feet seven inches, she carried enough extra pounds to make her look like most of the rest of the planet but not so many that she might stand out. Her hair, though looking a little lank today, was a nice shade of chestnut brown that probably caught the sun with lustre in better times and her chestnut brown eyes matched it perfectly even if they were puffy, red and swollen today.

'Thank you for coming so quickly, Mrs Fisher,' she said as we approached.

I extended my hand for her to shake. 'You are very welcome. Please call me Patricia. This is my associate, Jermaine.' I indicated to my left where he stood. She shook hands with him as well, glancing at his outfit but choosing to say nothing.

She invited us in, offering to make tea, which we declined, then leading us through to her lounge where we could all sit. I asked her to run through the circumstances of her husband's death again, taking out my own notepad this time; a trusted A5 pad with a ball point pen, not Jermaine's fancy electronic tablet.

'He often went climbing on a Sunday. I always go to church, but he refuses to come with me. He always said churches were for weddings and funerals and that now he was married he wasn't going back until he was dead. Unless my Susie got married, that is.'

I glanced around the room looking for pictures. 'How old is your daughter?'

'She's nineteen. She's a bit precocious at the moment. I'm having trouble keeping tabs on her. Or, at least, I was until Edward...' she let the sentence trail off, then restarted with a new one. 'What else do you need to know?'

My gaze was focused on a photograph of her daughter at what looked like a climbing event; she was wearing all the gear. 'Did your daughter climb?'

'Oh. Yes, she did. Ed got her into it. She was eight when I met him. Her dad left with another woman when she was tiny and never bothered with her, so it was nice that he took such an interest in her. He helped me raise her and she called him dad, never Ed. They did lots of stuff together.'

'I could do with a picture of your husband. Do you mind if I take this one?' I crossed the room to pluck it from the mantlepiece even as she worked out whether to say yes or not.

'Um, err, yes, of course. Whatever you need.'

'Where was she when it happened?' I asked.

Glumly, and with a touch of embarrassment, she admitted, 'With a boy.' I tilted my head slightly, hoping she would expand on her answer. 'It seems to be the thing these days. I thought my generation was sexually liberated but now the trend is to just find a boy and sleep with him when you feel inclined. I don't think she even learns their names half the time. I just beg her to be safe.'

'Do you know the boy's name on this occasion?'

'Harry, I think. She did tell me, but I wasn't really listening. The police quizzed her about where she was when Ed fell, that's how it came out. As soon as I said he had to have been murdered, the police started making enquiries, but they dismissed it within a couple of days.' She fell silent, as if contemplating something until I prompted her.

'You were telling us about Susie and the man she met? I take it they spent the night together.'

'Yes,' Sarah replied, her tone displaying her disappointment at her daughter's sexual freedom. 'She met him in a club in town on the Saturday night and spent the night at his place, somewhere near the river in town. She was still there when I called her to tell her what had happened. She's a good girl though, I suppose. She hasn't left my side since.'

'Where is she now?' I asked, challenging her last statement.

'She went to the funeral home this morning to start making arrangements. It ought to be me, but she insisted I let her do it.'

I changed tack. 'Tell me, Sarah, what do you think happened?'

She wriggled her lips around as she tried to find an answer. Her hands were in her lap, fidgeting around with a tissue and she stared at them rather than at Jermaine or me. 'I don't know,' she admitted finally, her eyes still on her lap until she said it, then she looked up at my face to convey how serious she was. 'I just know how careful he was about climbing. I couldn't possibly count the number of times he told Susie to check her equipment twice before setting off. Check it once, then check it again. You get one chance to get it wrong – that's what he always said. He was climbing the overhang at West Cliffe in Great Capwood Park when he fell. No one climbs that alone, especially not my Ed. Someone led him there, Mrs Fisher. They led him there and then they dropped him.'

Jermaine and I asked some more questions, taking notes as we built up a picture of Edward Foy's final movements. If Sarah was to be believed, his behaviour that morning was unusual. There appeared to be nothing else out of the ordinary though. He worked for a gas supplier as an engineer, not the sort of job that generated a lot of enemies. He didn't gamble, he didn't go out drinking with buddies and he was at home every evening, so Sarah was content to rule out the possibility that he was having an affair and fallen foul of another husband's anger.

The picture I had left me no clue whatsoever, but I would be chatting with DS Mike Atwell at four o'clock and might find out more then. Either Sarah Foy had it completely wrong and her husband was the victim of an unfortunate accident, or someone out there currently believed they had got away with murder. Either way, Mrs Foy was content to pay my fees, so I had a case to investigate.

She saw us to the door where Jermaine seemed very happy to discover a light drizzle had set in. His umbrella burst into life as the door closed behind us, his arm appearing for me to loop mine through so we could be close together under the shelter his umbrella provided on the way back to the car.

Interviewing Sarah had taken most of two hours, the question and answer session threatening to make me late for my next appointment with Emma Maynard and her dognapping case. A quick glance at the clock in my car reassured me that we would be there just about on time, so with thoughts of climbing and murder buzzing around my head, I set off to the next destination.

Dognapped

Emma Maynard lived in East Malling in one of the newer houses that the older members of the village denied were even part of it. Like all the greenbelt in the country, East and West Malling were victim to expansion, the government overruling planning restrictions to find land on which to build the tens of thousands of new houses the ever-growing population required.

The estate had been designed tastefully with a lake and a park, but the houses were small and far lower in price than the older properties in the village. Some claimed it lowered the overall value of any property in the village, most just complained about the additional cars on the roads and the extra kids hanging around at the weekends. There was a lot of snobbery in Kent's rural villages.

Her house was in a line of link detached houses, a term I always thought of as an oxymoron; how could they be called detached if they were linked to another house? It was pleasant looking enough, if barely bigger than a Victorian terraced house, and like Sarah Foy, Emma Maynard saw us coming and met us at her door. In her case, Emma's kitchen was at the front of the house and she appeared to have just finished washing up lunch things when we arrived.

Jermaine did the usual thing of getting my door and was clearly over the moon that it was still raining, opening his umbrella with a flourish.

'You look like John Steed,' commented Emma as we approached, a light frown creasing her forehead as she wondered why.

Jermaine just said, 'Thank you.'

Then I went through the introductions and before we knew it, we were sitting in a gallery. When she told me she worked from home, it sparked a speck of curiosity to know what she did. I would have asked at some point this afternoon, but I didn't have to because it was obvious she painted watercolours.

They were everywhere.

It was all English wild animals, hedgehogs, rabbits and hares, squirrels, badgers, and much more. Seeing us both looking, she explained, 'There's quite a market for my work. I'm really lucky. It's all I ever wanted to do.'

'You're very good,' I told her, not just because it seemed like the thing to say, but because it was true. I could imagine hanging some of her work in the manor house.

With a shrug, she said, 'Thank you.'

Then I noticed the section dedicated to dogs and there were a lot of paintings of a tiny teacup Yorkshire Terrier. I got down to business. 'I need to see the ransom message; can you forward it to me, please? Then I need to know what the police said, exactly when you noticed your dog was missing and how long after that the message arrived.'

Jermaine made sure she had the right number to send it to, the message popping up on my screen moments later.

Accompanying the message was a picture as proof of life showing Emma her dog. There were no clues in the background, no view out of a window we might be able to match to somewhere to narrow our search radius. The dog was inside a cardboard box that bore no markings and there was nothing else in the shot. The message was below it:

We have your dog. It will cost you ten thousand pounds to get him back. Get the money. Wait for further instructions.

I read it twice, then tried to work out what it told me. It was punctuated correctly and written in short, clipped sentences. I could draw a couple of different conclusions from it, the first was that it was written by someone English rather than one of the many millions of immigrants now living in the South of England. Such easy conclusions could easily be misleading though so I dismissed it and any others to wait until I knew more.

Horace, for that was the dog's name, was taken from the back garden, a small space with a five-foot fence, some time between one forty-five and two o'clock; she couldn't be more accurate than that. The back garden was completely secure; not a gap in the woodwork anywhere through which the dog could escape so the dognapper had to have opened the gate, snagged the dog and then made off with it. None of her neighbours had seen anyone acting in an unusual or suspicious manner or anyone that was new to the area. No one had seen anything, in fact. The dog was there one minute and gone the next.

It could be that a person walking by had chanced upon the dog and swiped it in an opportunistic crime, but how had they then got hold of Emma's mobile number? The answer to that question was that it is displayed on her website and on thousands of flyers and business cards, but the dognapper would still have to know who she was and that she had a dog.

'Do you have a partner?' Jermaine asked when I fell silent.

'You mean a business partner or a boyfriend?' she asked in reply, 'Because no to both, I think.'

'You think?' he repeated, looking up from his tablet.

I looked at her to see how she would answer. She shrugged. 'A definite no to the business partner. I sort of did have a boyfriend. I guess he was

26

more of a booty call than anything else, I met him on Tinder. His first name is Damian, but I don't know what his last name is. We never went out anywhere on a date,' she admitted as her cheeks reddened slightly. 'But I haven't heard from him in a while and he isn't answering his phone and I think he stole some money from me.'

Both Jermaine and I stared at her now. This could be a big fat clue. 'He took money. How much?' I asked.

'Just a few hundred. I often go to fayres and carnivals and farmers' markets. I sell quite a bit that way and it is almost always cash so I had a bundle of it in a plastic box in the drawer over there.' She pointed across the room and then walked to it to take out the box to show us. 'There was over a thousand here before but now there is less than seven hundred. No one else has been in the house in the last month except my mother and I don't think she took it.'

'Did he ever mention money? Was he broke?' That he never once took her out could be an indication that he was strapped for cash. Would he have stolen her dog believing she had the money to pay the ransom?

'No.' She looked like she was scouring her memory, questioning herself, but she decided, 'No. He was always well dressed, and he wore nice aftershave, the one that Jonny Marcone advertises...'

'Eau de Man,' supplied Jermaine.

'Who's Jonny Marcone?' I asked, feeling that I ought to know.

'A Hollywood A-lister, madam.' That made me feel better, I paid very little attention to movie stars or rock stars or any kind of stars for that matter. They were just people to me.

'Anyway,' Emma continued. 'I don't think he was short of money, but I think he took mine nevertheless.'

'Could he have stolen Horace?' I asked, watching to see her reaction. It had never occurred to her, both hands going to her mouth as she gasped at the very real possibility of it. 'He knows who you are, knows your phone number, and the dog would recognise him so might be more inclined to go to him when called.'

She already had her phone out and was trying to call his number. 'I'm going to kill him if he has my dog. It's one thing to sleep with me and decide to never call me again, but this is something else.' She waited impatiently for it to be answered and when it went to voice mail, she let his phone record some very choice words, mostly about what was going to happen to his genitalia if he had taken her dog.

'How long had you been seeing him?' asked Jermaine.

'Only about three weeks?' she replied.

Jermaine and I exchanged a glance. 'Long enough to win the dog's trust. Did he ever pay it much attention?' I asked.

'Oh, God, he never left it alone.' She looked angry now. Angry at herself mostly, I thought. 'Sometimes it was all I could do to get him to put Horace down and pay attention to me.'

I had what I felt was a really rude question to ask. 'Do you have the means to pay the ransom?'

Annoyed, she huffed out a breath. 'Yes and no. I can get it. I really want Horace back, but the police told me I shouldn't pay because, for one, they could just take him again, and, for two, I would then be funding a gang of criminals who would steal more dogs from other people. They are such scumbags. Now though, if it's Damian who has Horace, I might have to agree to pay just to lure him out.' She looked at the two of us. 'What do you think?'

It was a tough question. The concept of luring the dognapper out was appealing but I doubted the criminal would turn up in person, arranging some other devious method to obtain the cash and return the dog (or not) once they had it. I had to agree with the police; if none of the victims ever pay, the crime goes away, but there was no way of enforcing that.

Damian was a great starting point but as we pressed Emma for more information, she didn't have any. She didn't know his last name, or where he lived, or what he did for a living.

Unthinkingly, I asked, 'What on earth did you talk about then?'

Emma looked slightly embarrassed when she said, 'Um, we didn't really talk. I told you it was more of a booty call.' There was that phrase again. I had ignored it the first time, thinking I could ask Jermaine about it later, but he saw my forehead wrinkling now and leaned in to whisper in my ear. Now it was my turn to have red cheeks.

So Damian would turn up, have sex with her, play with the dog and then leave. And he did it during the day which to me suggested he had a wife and kids somewhere. Well, he wouldn't be the first person ever to live such a double life.

We went back around the subject of Horace the missing dog, Emma's habits and movements, Damian and her relationship with him, and a number of other elements of her life which may or may not prove to be connected, and accepted that we were not going to find out much more today. She didn't have a photograph of him, but we got a description, not that it was much to go on. He was a white man in his very early forties or thereabouts, a bit of salt and pepper around his temples but otherwise brown hair and he was average height and average build. He could be about half the men in England.

She signed her contract to engage me and transferred a deposit. I really wanted to catch whoever had her dog and that was what she employed me to do. Better to pay me some money than hand over ten grand to a criminal. Just like Sarah Foy, I needed to come through for her. At least this time I had a suspect even if I didn't know anything worthwhile about him.

Next on my list was afternoon tea with my tame detective. I offered to drop Jermaine back at the house as I was heading to West Malling High Street, but he wanted to go to the drycleaners there with some of his uniforms. Apparently, they were already in the boot of my car.

Teatime

Mike Atwell was already sitting with a newspaper and a glass of water when I arrived. I recognised his socks which is a dangerous thing to say about a man. It's a lot like saying you recognise their underwear, but in Mike's case, he had a penchant for wearing garish socks. Today's were bright, and I mean bright, red. They were the same shade as a harlot's knickers, that's how red they were. He had the broadsheet paper covering his face and his legs stretched out to show the shock of red between shoes and trousers. I stopped at his table and hooked two fingers over the top of his paper to pull it down.

'Oh, hello, Patricia,' he said, returning my smile as he folded the paper. 'Just catching up on the news.'

'Anything interesting?' I asked to make conversation.

'Goodness, no,' he chuckled. 'It's all nonsense about one celebrity or another.' He caught the eye of a waitress who was hovering and waiting for him to signal. Our order was simple. They make a tea platter for two which contains some small, but very nicely presented sandwiches, plus a selection of small cakes which is then followed by warm fruit scones served with clotted cream and jam. It sounds like a lot but is a sensible afternoon portion when shared. They also have a savoury platter with cheese scones and one can substitute the pot of tea for a bottle of wine, but we stuck with the traditional offering.

Once the order was placed, Mike got straight down to business. 'Derek Quince confessed everything once he was at the station, not that we really needed a confession, but it works in his favour at trial if he cooperates.'

'What will he receive?' I asked, curious to hear what the penalty for sending threatening and unpleasant letters might be.

'Probably probation,' he replied. 'It's a first offense, no one was hurt, and he is unlikely to commit any further crimes. He could get up to six months, but I don't think we could find a judge willing to issue that sentence.'

It didn't seem like much. The vicar would reverse his decision and reinstate both Fothergills, I was sure, but they had forked out to hire me to clear their names. The criminal prosecution system wasn't set up to help people get their money back though so they would have to pursue him for damages if they wanted to recoup their loss. None of that was anything to do with me but I knew these people and saw them most weeks.

Our food arrived, Mike doing the duty with the pot of tea to fill our cups as I selected a smoked salmon sandwich.

'What can you tell me about Edward Foy's death?' I asked once the first delicious morsel was gone.

'There isn't much to tell; that's what I can tell you.' He sipped his tea, then took out a notebook. 'I went to the station today to speak with a counterpart there.' He took reading glasses from an inside pocket, slipped them on and started reading. 'Edward Foy was found by Simon Wessex and his wife Maria when they arrived at Great Capwood Park for a planned day of climbing. They are members of the West Kent Climbing Society and were to be met there by a dozen other people. None of them got to climb of course because we shut the whole area off.'

I took another look at the tray, selecting an egg and cress finger sandwich before offering him the platter. I was hungrier than I expected to be and wanted to make sure I didn't eat the lot while he was talking.

With a ham and mustard sandwich in his right hand, he held the notepad with his left and continued to talk, poking the air with the sandwich for effect every now and then. 'He was pronounced dead at the scene, death being attributed to massive internal haemorrhaging and loss of blood. He fell more than three hundred feet they estimate, landing on the rocks below. Their estimate coming from the height where they found the broken piece of equipment; something called a quickdraw. He took a small bite of his sandwich and chewed it as he read his notes. 'They did their best to keep foot traffic to a minimum, but the area is well used by climbers. They found his footprints though. They lead away from his car and there was no set coming from the passenger side and no fresh tyre tracks, so they don't think there were any other cars there.'

'The conclusion being that he arrived alone, climbed alone, and therefore his death was an accident caused by a piece of faulty equipment.'

'Exactly,' he agreed. 'They had a quick delve into his past, but short of inventing a conspiracy theory, he had nothing going on in his life that might attract a murderer.'

'His wife feels otherwise.'

'So I understand. It was remarked upon that only a fool would climb the route he took without someone to belay.'

I shook my head as I frowned. I knew what belaying was, one person climbs while the other stays on the ground using a rope to support them should they fall. Not possible on a mountainside, but on a hobby slope, there was usually a walking route to the top where a rope could be secured. Then, in the event of a fall, the belayer would catch the climber.

'Surely, if someone wanted him dead, they would only need to offer to belay, and then, when he slipped, they could let go of the rope. Edward

33

would crash to the ground hundreds of feet below.' I mimed falling and going splat.

Mike shrugged. 'That sounds like a solid theory until one takes into account that there is only one set of footprints. Plus, the killer would have to rely on the climber actually falling, because, what if he didn't? Then what? Also, the broken quickdraw was three hundred feet up but still two hundred feet from the top and right on the edge of an overhang. That can't have been easy to get to if we are suggesting someone planted it there.'

I sighed deeply. It was a taxing mystery already and I hadn't even started looking into it yet. I thought of something. 'The body was released today, what about the evidence? They must have taken a load from the scene; the broken quickdraw and his ropes.'

'Yes. No doubt they did. They won't want to keep it now they have decided there is no crime to investigate. I'll look into where it is and when it will be released to the family. Often, the families don't want things like that back because it just serves as a reminder.'

The sandwiches were gone, nothing but a few crumbs to show they were ever there. 'Would you like a cake?' I offered him first choice.

He took a finger sized cream slice and did his best to bite into it without sending crumbs everywhere. He did a terrible job. It was the one cake I hoped he would take because, while tasty, it is just fresh cream and flaky pastry; a guaranteed mess. He had a blob of cream on his tie.

'I have another case to look into, actually,' I announced between bites. 'It a dognapping case. Do the police get many incidents of pets being held to ransom? Is there a gang operating in the area that you know of?'

He gave my question some thought, screwing up his face as he wracked his brains. 'You know, I don't remember the last case of dognapping. It must be three or four years ago. You say you have one now?'

'Yes, out in East Malling. A woman had her little Yorkie stolen and a ransom on a text message an hour later. They want ten grand but haven't been back in touch to tell her where to take it. The number was hidden, of course.'

'Did she report it?'

'Yes, she got a squad car from Maidstone by the sound of it. The officers were helpful enough, I think, but told her not to pay.'

He nodded, pursing his lips and looking sad. 'That is the best advice. Unfortunately, the way to diffuse this sort of crime is to make it profitless. The dogs turn up sometimes, the criminals not actually ruthless enough to kill them. We encourage people to make sure their pets are microchipped. Beyond that, it is quite difficult to catch the perpetrators.'

I could offer no argument. I had two good cases. Both suggesting a level of difficulty I ought to relish but also worried might prove too much. Once our tray of cakes was reduced to jam smears and the pot of tea drained of its final dregs, I thanked him for his time, he thanked me for the tea, and we promised to get together again soon.

I needed to get home, because, on top of everything else, my good friend Lady Mary Bostihill-Swank was due to arrive at my house shortly. She hadn't seen it yet, having been out of the country with her best-selling novelist husband for the last few weeks as he toured America promoting his latest book which was being turned into a film starring an actor who Lady Mary described as a man-sized lollipop. I wasn't entirely sure what that description was meant to impart, and I chose to not ask.

Whatever the case, she would arrive soon, would expect gin to flow from the taps and I knew Jermaine had been annoying the cook, Mrs Ellis, to ensure the meal she prepared was going to be to his standard.

He would be there now, butlering around in his tails, enjoying his position as head of the staff even though I insisted he was my friend and I didn't need a butler.

I checked the clock on the wall as I left, smiling to myself as I mimicked Lady Mary's voice, 'Goodness, Patricia, look, it's gin o'clock.'

Lady Mary

'Patricia, sweetie, you have such a beautiful home,' Lady Mary gushed. 'You have such a knack for landing on your feet.'

I found her sitting in my study, the room in which I am beginning to amass case notes and gradually turn into a home office. It is far bigger than the office in Rochester, as are some of the wardrobes in my bedroom, so it makes sense to use it for most of my work, reserving the office for a professional business address and client meeting point. I think inviting clients to the grand manor house would scare many of them away.

Lady Mary got up as I came into the room, placing her goblet of gin and tonic down to greet me. I didn't ask if it was her first or fifth drink, whatever number it was seemed irrelevant to her level of sobriety, which was always slightly sloshed but never actually wobbly, and besides, she probably had four at lunchtime anyway.

Lady Mary Bostihill-Swank is the owner of a wildlife park a few miles away and does very well for herself. An eccentric grandfather created the park in the 1920s, making a lot of money from it. Today, it continues to thrive, and she married a fledgling author who went on to make millions for himself. She was never going to be short on money. At fifty-seven, she was just a few years older than me and we had quite similar world views. We bonded on board over mutual local knowledge and gin. Mostly gin, in fact, and then bonded even more when some gangsters tried to kill us both. She was skinny as a rake, probably because she drank all her calories and posher than gold embossed toilet paper.

We hugged briefly. 'It's a bit more than I need,' I admitted. 'I am still getting used to it. It's only been two days since I last got lost.' She laughed at me, but I wasn't exaggerating. 'Honestly, I have been thinking about marking the walls so I can find my way around. Breadcrumbs wouldn't work because Anna would eat them.'

'Yes, talking of dogs, where is your little ankle biter? You said she had her puppies?'

I wanted to see her too. The arrival of her puppies kept her at home, so my adventures were not currently complicated by the addition of an aggressive miniature Dachshund. I missed her company though and there is nothing in the world like a puppy cuddle.

We found them in the pantry, which is a large room just off the main kitchen. I say main kitchen because there is another, smaller one, in each of the wings so the family, if one had sufficient members to fill the house, would not need to call down to the kitchen for a snack if one wanted popcorn or a sandwich or a can of soda one evening.

The pantry didn't actually contain any food, that being its original purpose. Designed to be a cold store when the house was built long before refrigerators, it was no longer efficient for keeping food in and now stored kitchen equipment instead. Anna had a large basket set to one side and a flap to give her access to the garden when she wanted.

She also had access to the kitchen which I expected to be a problem for the cook, Mrs Ellis, but she liked the company it seemed. I just hoped there weren't too many dropped titbits.

Anna's head popped up as we came into the room. She saw me and abandoned her four tiny puppies as she leapt out to scurry across the room for a pick up. 'Hello, Anna,' I cooed at her as she tried to lick my face. I nuzzled her neck and told her what a clever girl she was for the millionth time.

Lady Mary spied the wriggling bag of snakes that was Anna's puppies and fell upon them, trying to balance all four on her lap as she got into the basket with them. 'Oh, my goodness, Patricia, they are adorable.'

Squinting to see which one she had in her hands, I said, 'That's Ringo. On your knee is Paul and trying to bite your arm is John. The little one still trying to climb on you is Georgie. She's the only girl.'

Mrs Ellis came across to see us, wiping her hands on her pinafore as she came into the pantry. 'Do you ladies have everything you need?' she asked.

I smiled at her, buoyed by the joy that is puppies, 'Yes, yes, Pam. How are you?'

'Oh, mustn't grumble.' It was her standard reply. I don't think she ever considered the question, when I, or anyone else, asked it, firing off her standard response each time. 'Will you be taking dinner in the dining room, Mrs Fisher?'

'Pam you can call me Patricia, you know. Hearing someone call for Mrs Fisher makes me look about for my mother-in-law.'

'That just wouldn't be right, Mrs Fisher,' she argued.

Internally I sighed. The house came with a staff of seven, each of them with a specific task to perform. Every one of them addressed me as Mrs Fisher or madam, no doubt Jermaine's doing as head of the staff. I should probably be thankful none of them ever tried to curtsy.

I replied to her question. 'There's a small room at the back of the house which overlooks the garden.'

'The billiards room?' Mrs Ellis asked for confirmation.

'Why would it be called the billiards room?'

'Because Lord Etherington, who owned the house before the Maharaja bought it in the seventies, used to have billiards tables in there.'

I stared at her. 'Pam, how long have you worked here?'

'I started right after school in 1981 but my mother was the cook before me, so I joined her as a kitchen hand when I was twelve in 1975.' Right, well that explained why she knew so much about the place.

'Super. I think we'll be in there, thank you.' Mrs Ellis bustled off to get on with whatever she was doing, and we decided to take Anna, the puppies and their basket back to where we would be more comfortable.

On our way to the billiards room, a shout made us turn our heads, 'Hey, ladies.' It was Barbie, my perfectly proportioned, tall, lean, blonde gym instructor friend from Los Angeles. She and I met on the Aurelia the morning after I boarded the ship. She was Jermaine's BFF and the two of them were inseparable. Faced with a heartbroken, slightly podgy, but above all self-loathing middle-aged woman, the two of them had helped me turn my life around, Barbie choosing to beat me into shape and help me find the strength to love myself instead of caring too much about the size of my bum. As a side effect, my bum shrank anyway. She had a Japanese boyfriend who was a junior doctor at St Barts in London and the two of them lived with me because I wanted to keep my friends close.

'Is it gin o'clock?' she asked Lady Mary, chuckling at her own joke as she used Lady Mary's favourite expression.

Of course, Lady Mary didn't understand that it was a joke, since gin is serious business for her. 'I dare say it is, sweetie, I'm parched. Shall we find that lazy butler friend of yours and see if we can scare up a few glasses?'

40

Barbie joined us for one, which she sipped before departing to get showered and changed. Hideki, her doctor boyfriend, didn't get home every day, his shift pattern made that impossible, but he was on his way now and they were still in the heady crush of early love where locked doors were a must, but clothes were entirely optional.

'Patricia tells me you found work,' said Lady Mary as Jermaine handed out glasses.

Barbie took a sip of her beverage, savouring the complex flavours before she answered. 'Yes, Mary. There's a big health centre a couple of miles away. I work there.'

Lady Mary smiled at her and turned to me. 'And you have your own detective business now.'

'Private investigations,' I corrected her.

'What's the difference?' she asked with a frown.

'Well,' I took a sip of my gin and put the glass down. 'The difference is subtle but important. The term detective is most often associated with law enforcement and as such police detectives do nothing but investigate crimes. A private investigator will, however, take on public sector work and may be hired by an individual. The nature of the investigation may not be criminal at all; I could be hired to track down a missing spouse for instance.'

'I see,' said Lady Mary.

Barbie asked, 'Have you ever had a job, Mary?'

Lady Mary almost spat out her gin as she shuddered. 'Heavens no, girl. What an awful thought. My father wanted me to train as a veterinarian but fortunately for me I am simply not bright enough to pass the entrance exams. I have always stuck with what I am good at.'

'And what's that?' I asked.

'Drinking, my dear, drinking.' She held up her glass in salute, then knocked it back in one like a shot. 'I dare say I might have a case for you though, sweetie.'

'Oh yes?' Both Barbie and I leaned forward to listen as Lady Mary told us she was missing several small trinkets and couldn't work out what had happened to them. She wanted to be clear that she wasn't reporting a theft, at least she didn't think she was. In fact, she told us she held off from saying anything to anyone out of worry that she might be getting a bit senile and would be shown that she had absentmindedly put them in the freezer or something.

'It's not something I want you to look into straight away,' she told us. 'Maybe keep it in mind, Patricia, if you have a really slow week and need something to do.'

The conversation turned to her husband and his latest book, the film they were making of it and where he was currently. Barbie finished her drink and left us just as dinner arrived and the evening passed pleasantly until, with a yawn, Lady Mary asked her driver to take her home. It had been good to have a friend who wasn't intimidated by the house and the wealth. I had definitely imbibed at least one more gin and tonic than was sensible though and made my way to bed concerned for what Barbie might make me do to burn it off the next day.

Exercise and Research

At six the next morning, I met Barbie in the entrance lobby of my house. She was performing yoga poses as she waited for me to arrive, looking balanced and serene and perfect. I glanced in the big mirror to find my hair was sticking out at angles, I had creases in my face where it had been stuck to the material of my pillows all night, and my head split into an enormous and uncontrollable yawn.

Yeah, I was ready.

Barbie's life was all about exercise and eating well and being healthy. She would create macrobiotic things in the kitchen and keep them in the fridge where I swear they came to life. Apparently, they were incredible for one's gut, if one could get past the smell; which I couldn't. She had brought exercise into my life though, which I was grateful for. I wasn't feeling particularly grateful as we set off into the gloomy morning air, the sun also feeling too tired to make it out of bed at this time. It was cool out; cool enough to make me wish I had gloves but not so cold that I actually needed them. I knew there was no sense in telling Barbie I felt cold; she would take that as a cue to run faster because that would generate heat.

Forty-five minutes later, we arrived back at the house, slowing to a walk for the final few hundred yards. Barbie looked almost exactly the same as she had when we set off, the only sign that she had done anything were a few beads of perspiration on her brow. I looked like I had fallen into a cow trough. There were bits of twig in my hair from low hanging branches which never touched Barbie even though she was taller than me and I had mud up my shins, seemingly finding every puddle while Barbie somehow floated over them.

'How do you do that?' she asked, taking in my battered appearance as I tried to get a thorny piece of bramble out of my own blonde locks.

'It's a skill,' I replied flippantly, finally tugging it free with an, 'Ouch.'

We both went inside for a shower, though she barely appeared to need one. While we were jogging, I distracted myself by considering the day ahead and the two cases I wanted to focus on. The first thing I planned to do after breakfast was visit the local post office where I would ask some questions of the village busybody, Mavis.

Mavis knew everyone and everything about everyone. Over several decades she had made it her mission to know all the dirty secrets in the village, going out of her way to embellish stories if they weren't juicy enough. The post office was in West Malling's sister village, East Malling, just a couple of miles away. I could walk there, but it was a little far to walk Anna both ways so I would park at the post office and walk a circuit from there to make sure my dog got her morning exercise.

The post office didn't open until nine though, so I had more than two hours to kill, some of which I filled with research. Barbie joined me; she was more efficient at it and we had discussed it as we ran which had piqued her interest.

Arriving in my new study/office with her hair looking perfect and a fresh set of gym clothes on, she slid into the chair at the computer desk, fired it into life and called me over to see.

'This is a quickdraw,' she said. Jermaine had already shown me what one looked like, but she seemed to know more about the subject, telling me she used to climb a lot in California growing up because there were lots of great places to climb. 'You use it when you are leading a climb. So, for Edward Foy, who was climbing alone, he would have placed an anchor

44

into a crevice and then clipped the quickdraw to the anchor and then clipped his rope into it.'

'What's the rope for?'

'To catch you if you fall. He would have needed a self-belay setup but by clipping in every few yards, you limit the distance you will fall if you lose your grip.'

I ran through the mental image in my head. 'His quickdraw failed, and he fell three hundred feet. Wouldn't he have only fallen to the next lowest arrest point?'

Barbie's eyes locked with mine. 'Totally, unless he was being really lazy and had only clipped in to one point. That would be dangerous but there are a lot of free climbers out there now; climbers who want the ultimate experience by using no safety equipment.'

'Isn't that just asking to die?' I asked, startled by the concept.

She shrugged. 'Lots of them do every year. That's how they know it is extreme climbing.'

'How often do things like quickdraws fail?'

'Almost never. But nothing lasts forever, so if it was old or had been damaged and he continued to use it, at some point it would break just like anything else.'

I pursed my lips at that point. His wife, Sarah, was insistent that he was safety conscious and always checked his equipment, replacing it regularly. He climbed with his daughter so I needed to find her; she might have a different story than the one he told his wife. Maybe he *was* a risk taker. Maybe he only pretended to spend the money on new equipment while secretly spending it on something else. He wouldn't be the first husband, or wife for that matter, I had come across who was believed to be a wonderful, faithful person when secretly they were an utter scumbag.

I murmured, 'I need to speak to his daughter.'

'Susie?' asked Barbie, getting my attention because I hadn't told her the girl's name yet. Barbie was on social media though, delving into the family life.

I looked over her shoulder, seeing the girl from the photograph with Edward, her stepdad. Barbie had her photo albums open and was scrolling through them, finding lots of pictures of Susie as a teenage girl with her friends, with her mum and Edward on holiday, going climbing, and more recently, pictures of her with women and men her own age, clearly out drinking and partying.

It all seemed very normal. Her relationship status was listed as single, which matched what her mother described.

'I can message her from here, if you want to make contact?' Barbie offered. 'She might answer straight away. It's a Tuesday, so she will have classes if she is at university.' I could see she was listed as attending the University of Greenwich, which I knew to have campuses spread all over Kent.

'Sure. Introduce me, please, and let her know I am looking into her step-father's death.'

Her fingers flew over the keyboard. 'Anything else?'

I had to think about that. I wasn't sure what else I could research; I had so little to go on in both cases. 'Can you look at Emma Maynard? She's a local artist but I am more interested in her social life. She had a boyfriend who wasn't a boyfriend...'

'Booty call?'

'Apparently. Her little dog got stolen and then she got a ransom note, but everything points to her booty call/boyfriend as the culprit.'

Her search brought up several Emma Maynards, which forced me to scrutinise the pictures to determine which one I wanted. Her social media profile didn't tell me much either.

The computer pinged. 'Susie replied already,' said Barbie, moving the mouse to click on the message. 'She wrote, "Dad died in an accident. Please stop taking my mother's money, you cadaverous old cow." That's not very nice.'

'No. It's not,' I agreed. It wasn't the reaction I expected, that was for sure. 'Let's brush over the horrible insult. Can you reply with; Did Edward often climb alone?'

The message pinged off into the ether, and a moment later, a reply returned. It contained just two words, the first starting with an F.

'I don't think I am going to get much out of Susie over the internet. Perhaps I will do better face to face.' I was talking to myself but as I said the words, I wondered if I would need some kind of leverage or inside information in order to get her to talk. Tracking her down just to get the same two-word answer to my face would be a waste of effort and time. She had to know about her stepfather's climbing habits though. If he often climbed alone and didn't take care of his equipment the way Sarah believed he did then I could reasonably arrive at the same conclusion as the police, close the case and tell Mrs Foy that I too believed his death was accidental. Explaining that her picture of his safety habit was false ought to at least give her closure. If, however, Susie agreed with her mother, then murder looked more and more likely.

47

'This one and the dognapping both sound like tough cases,' Barbie said, getting out of her chair to stretch in place. 'I'm going to leave you to have fun with them. I have a class to teach in thirty minutes and I need to get it set up.' I had attended some of Barbie's classes in the past, making the mistake of thinking I would be able to keep up with the other people. Her bodypump class almost killed me. On her way to the door, she turned to walk backwards, 'If you need me to help with anything, just let me know.'

In the silence of the room, I tried to lay out the cases on paper. Making two separate lists for each, I wrote down facts pertaining to each case and then a list of questions. One thing was for certain; I didn't know much, and I had a lot of questions.

The Village

After a vegetable omelette for breakfast and a stiff, dark cup of coffee, I took Anna away from her puppies for some exercise of her own. It was nearing nine o'clock, so by the time I had given her a decent walk, the post office would be open.

I parked in the small carpark outside, taking care to avoid puddles as Tom, the handyman at the house, cleaned my car each time I returned it. It was always spotless, which I admit I love, but I didn't want to fall into the habit of not caring about it getting dirty just because it wasn't my task to clean it.

Anna pulled at the lead excitedly as soon as her paws hit the dirt. Her tail shot bolt upright, a sure sign that she had seen something to chase, and as I followed her gaze, I saw a squirrel halfway down a tree on the opposite side of the road. It was staring back at her. The squirrel mafia were a surprise to me. I always thought of squirrels as timid, harmless little things who lived in trees and wouldn't hurt a fly. Anna saw them differently and I wasn't so sure she had it wrong. Watching them from the house as she ran around barking beneath them, I had a growing concern that they were organised. Anna was Eliot Ness of the Untouchables and the squirrel mafia ran circles around her. Now the two of them were locked in a stare-down contest and I found myself waiting to see which of them would blink first.

'Morning, Mrs Fisher.'

The sudden voice behind me made my heart jump a beat and caused me to squeal with fright. As my heart restarted, I whipped around to find Sam Chalk giving me a curious look.

'Everything alright, Mrs Fisher?' he asked innocently.

'Oh, yes,' I gasped, getting my breath back. 'Just peachy. Do you have to sneak up on people?'

Sam Chalk grinned a broad, goofy grin. He was the only child of Melissa and Paul Chalk, a couple I knew from my childhood. Paul's younger sister, Cynthia had been in my year at school, but Melissa and I bonded more than thirty years ago when we both arrived for a check-up at the doctors sporting worthwhile baby bumps. We were due a day apart. She gave birth to Sam the following April. I lost mine two days after I saw her that day. Sam was born with Downs Syndrome, something a lot of people in the village treated as if it were a disease, shying away from him whenever he came near. He lacked the ability to communicate clearly, his mental age stuck in single figures though he was in his thirties now, but I had always thought he was a sweet boy.

'Can I stroke your dog?' he asked, ignoring my question about sneaking.

I smiled and pulled Anna back gently toward me. She didn't want to come; she wanted to kill the squirrel and was rather put out that I was making her lose the staring contest.

'This is Anna,' I told him as I picked her up. Her paws were dirty but I had on a Barbour wax jacket so the dirt wouldn't penetrate the fabric or stick to it.

'She looks like a sausage,' he laughed, stroking her ears.

'Yes, she's a miniature Dachshund. They get called sausage dogs because of their long bodies. She just had puppies,' I told him remembering something he would undoubtedly find interesting. 'I can message your mum to bring you around to see them if you like.'

'That's okay,' he glanced at me with a smile. 'I see a puppy every day. It lives in a shed near me.'

'You're here early,' said Mavis. I saw her appear around the side of the post office a few seconds ago and missed what Sam said. I figured he would be excited to see the puppies so I would message Melissa later. I was sure I still had her number somewhere but if not, I knew where she lived and could just knock on the door. Mavis came to stand with Sam and me. 'Is there something you need desperately or are you just taking the dog for a walk? Hello, Sam,' she said, making sure she acknowledged the man I was talking to.

'Both. I have a question for you about Emma Maynard.' Now I had her attention. She loved the opportunity to gossip, so I was going to give her something juicy to chew on and see if I couldn't get some information out of her.

Her face betraying her instant interest, Mavis said, 'Ooh, go on, what's the question?'

'Don't you need to open the post office?' I asked, seeing a woman heading down the road towards us. The post office was the only thing in this direction so she had to be coming here and there would be plenty more along soon I felt sure.

'Nah, stuff 'em,' Mavis replied, reminding me how little she cared about actually doing her job, the gossip probably being the only thing that got her to turn up at all.

A second glance revealed that the woman now closing in on our position was Angelica Howard-Box, a woman I went to school with many years ago who had ideas above her station back then and hadn't changed since. She was one of the girls at school whose father had money and she was only too happy to let us all know it. She and I had a long-standing

51

rivalry which started over a boy when we were eight-years-old and was yet to be settled. I agreed with Mavis – stuff her. She could wait.

Turning my attention back to Mavis, I said, 'Emma Maynard's little dog was stolen a couple of days ago.'

'I know where there's a little dog,' said Sam, continuing to stroke Anna. Neither Mavis nor I paid him any attention.

'What, little Horace?' Of course Mavis knew who I was talking about; she knew everyone in the village.

'Yes. Whoever took him then demanded a ransom for his return, but I think it might be a gentleman who had been calling on her during the day.'

Mavis frowned. 'Like... like for a booty call?' There was the expression again. How come everyone on the planet knew the term booty call but me?

I pressed on. 'Yes, exactly like that. He got friendly with the dog and he had her number and knew when and how to grab the dog. Also, he stopped calling and will not now answer his phone when she calls it.'

'Ah,' said Mavis knowingly. 'He'll have a burner phone. A special one for talking to his ladies that his wife doesn't know about.' Mavis certainly knew her stuff. Anna wriggled in my arms; the squirrel was back, and she wanted to get down.

'That might well be the case. Anyway, I am trying to get her dog back for her and I don't have much to go on.' I described the man as Emma had described him to me. 'Have you seen anyone like that in the shop? A man who popped in during the day but hasn't been in for a week now?'

She thought about it.

Over at the door to the post office, Angelica Howard-Box said, 'Ahem.' Quite loudly. I heard her, turning my head and giving her a smile I didn't mean. Mavis blanked her completely.

'I don't think I can pinpoint anyone who that might be,' said Mavis slowly. 'I do have CCTV footage from inside the post office backed up though so if Emma wants to look through it, maybe she can identify him.'

'That's a great idea!' It really was. I certainly hadn't thought of it. I would call her shortly and see what I could arrange. 'How about people that live near her? I wondered if you might be able to ask if anyone saw him coming or going. Maybe someone saw his car; just knowing what kind of car he has could help. All I have at the moment is a first name – Damian, but that could easily be made up.'

'Leave it with me, Patricia,' Mavis grinned. 'I shall be sure to find out what there is to know.'

'Ahem,' said Angelica. She wasn't waiting over by the shop anymore; she was invading our personal space. She hadn't counted on Anna though who was still ferociously committed to defending me and saw Angelica's proximity as a threat.

As she snarled and lunged at Angelica's feet, I did nothing at all to stop her. I even considered letting the lead fall from my hands so Anna could claw at Angelica's boots.

She leapt out of the way, 'Good grief!' she exclaimed in startled surprise. 'What a vicious little beast.'

I scooped Anna into my arms as she continued to bark and fight to get to the perceived attacker. 'She's nothing of the sort, Angelica. She's just a good judge of character.'

Narrowing her eyes at me, Angelica turned her head to look at Mavis. 'Shouldn't you be opening the post office, Mavis? You have customers waiting.'

Mavis chuckled. 'Not anyone important though, is it?' Then she toddled off toward the shop with a cackle, holding out her hand to take Sam's, 'Come along, Sam. Did mum send you with a list?' They were gone, which left Angelica fuming and staring at me.

'I heard you were back,' she said. I could tell she was working up to an insult, but I let it come, too bored and too disinterested to care what she said. 'Poor, Patricia,' Angelica made a sympathetic face. 'Couldn't satisfy your man so he ran off with the village trollop. That must be so embarrassing.'

'Not really. He wasn't a very good husband.'

Unwilling to be put off in her desire to be unpleasant, she kept going, 'But now you have to get a divorce and find a job and find a place to live; such trying times.' She made herself look utterly depressed about my situation. A smile cracked my face as I realised she didn't know. She lived so far above the other villagers with her head in the sky that she didn't know I lived in a seventy-three-room manor house and had a booming business of my own.

Well, I wasn't going to be the one to tell her.

I smiled again, beginning to walk away with Anna as I said, 'I already have a place. It's not much, but I'll get by.' I didn't leave her space to add anything else, heading across the road and into the woods so Anna could run and explore, but when I looked back, I saw her frowning at my Aston Martin and wondering who owned it.

Investigating

The first thing I did was call Emma and explain to her about the CCTV footage at the post office. The concept of spotting the man she knew clearly excited her, so she was going straight there, she said. I could feel the case moving forward and just knew we were going to catch the perpetrator. I asked Emma to call me if she found him; I would need to then use the footage and my friendly detective sergeant to get a name and then an address.

In contrast, getting an address for Simon and Maria Wessex, the couple who found Edward Foy's body that fateful morning, was easy; I asked Jermaine to do it. Just as adept as Barbie, he cross referenced what he knew about them with the phone book and an address finder and there it was.

He was more... what? I didn't want to use the word sensible when I described his attire today when compared with the Steed outfit from yesterday, so perhaps sombre would have to do. He was more sombrely dressed today in a navy-blue suit with tan brogues. His slightly flamboyant nature wasn't to be completely quelled though so his jacket's collar was leopard print. Navy-blue leopard print, but leopard print, nevertheless. His tie matched it.

Yet again he wanted to accompany me, and I could see no reason to dissuade him. The Aston Martin was pressed into action once more as I pointed it in the general direction of Sandwich. Sandwich is yet another wonderful and quaint, small town on the southeast coast. A medieval embankment, built to keep ancient marauders out, can still be followed all the way around the town though the houses, which would once have all been inside the embankment for protection, have now spread beyond it. I hadn't been there in years, there having been no reason to visit it, but I remembered the road layout when I arrived.

Simon and Maria were not at home, but they owned a shop selling camping, sailing, and outdoor gear in Sandwich's small town centre; we found them there, both conducting a stock take when we went in.

'Hello,' said a man sitting on the floor at the foot of a rack of climbing harnesses. I recognised him from the profile Jermaine showed me, and also the woman standing above him with a clip board. 'One moment, please,' he begged as he continued counting, reached a total and had his wife note it.

She said, 'Sorry. It was really quiet in the shop today, so we thought we would get this done now rather than wait until closing and do it then. We do most of our trade via the internet these days. It seems hardly anyone wants to go to a shop to buy what they need.'

Simon clambered to his feet. 'Are you just nosing around Sandwich and thought you would pop in, or are you serious outdoorsy types with something particular in mind? All are welcome, of course,' he added quickly. He addressed Jermaine in favour of me, probably deciding that I didn't look like the outdoor type at all in my Chanel jacket.

Jermaine said, 'Actually, sir, we are here to speak to you about Edward Foy. You are familiar with his name?' When a little of the colour drained out of Simon's face, Jermaine indicated to his right where I was standing, drawing Simon's eyes to look at me. 'I have the honour of naming Mrs Patricia Fisher. Mrs Fisher has been engaged to investigate his death.'

The honour of naming? Being with Jermaine really was like hanging out in the 18th century sometimes.

I stepped forward with my hand extended. Simon took it but his grip was weak, his fingers doing little more than wiping against mine. He looked a little sick and a little nervous though I had no idea why. As his hand fell away, I said, 'Hello, Simon.' Then I shook hands with his wife

56

Maria, who just looked curious to hear what we had to say. 'Hello, Maria. I am hoping to ask you a few questions, that's all. I am building a picture of what might have happened to him.'

Jermaine pulled out his tablet and poised his fingers ready to make notes.

Simon licked his lips nervously.

'Is there something bothering you?' I asked him. 'You look worried.'

'Um, no. No. I just don't like being asked about dead people that's all. What is it you want to know?'

Maria spoke up. 'We've both been having trouble sleeping, truth be told. Our business is all about promoting climbing and outdoor pursuits, we sold him half of the items he used that day. I guess... I guess we've been waiting for someone to point the finger at us and try to say it's our fault his equipment failed even though it all comes with manufacturers guarantees and we only sell it.'

Now I understood. It was their livelihood they feared. That they sold him a lot of the gear was interesting though. 'You sold to him, so you knew him in person?'

Simon answered, 'He came in the shop a couple of times a year and we saw him at meets occasionally. We are on some of the same social media groups and might speak online a few times a year. I guess you could say we knew of each other but that was about it.'

'Do you have a record of what you sold him?'

A look flashed between them. 'Yes,' said Maria, already moving to the computer. 'Why hadn't I thought of that? He bought most of it via our website, so he has a customer file.' With a few clicks she had his file up and turned the screen so we could see it. 'Here you go.' Then, with a finger, she traced down the list of purchases, which went back several years. 'Here's the last set of quickdraws he bought back in June.' On the screen, not that I really knew what I was looking at, was an entry for quickdraws with a part number and a date of purchase. It meant he bought new ones; it didn't mean he used them.

'Can you print that, please?' asked Jermaine.

'Of course.' Maria clicked a key and somewhere behind the counter a printer came to life.

It was a good idea to take the list. Maybe we could perform an inventory of equipment later – see if there were items missing and what the general condition was.

I pressed on with a new question, 'Did you recognise him when you found him?'

Simon shook his head and looked at the ground. This time it was Maria to provide the answer. 'We just knew it was a climber in trouble. He landed face down on the rocks and there was too much blood for us to see who it was.'

'He was quite misshapen,' added Simon.

I didn't want to dwell on the state of Edward's body. I could only imagine what falling that kind of distance might do. I went back to the equipment. 'You were the first on the scene. Did you see anyone else there, or any sign that anyone else had been there?'

Once again, Simon shook his head. 'No. The police asked the same question. It was still quite early in the morning. He must have got there as the sun came up, which isn't a good idea because the rocks still have dew on them. Climbing alone... it's fraught with risk without unnecessarily adding yet more. We called for paramedics and the police turned up with them when we said the faller was definitely dead. They inspected the scene straight away and asked about other people. His car was there, but there were clearly only one set of prints leading from the driver's door, the ground in the parking area is soft enough to leave footprints.'

'You knew him a little from social media and the climbing community; do you recall him ever talking about free-climbing?'

Simon and Maria exchanged a glance to confirm before he said, 'No. No, I don't think he ever did. We talked about that when the police checked his ID at the scene, and we realised who it was. The free climbers are a different bunch but that doesn't mean he wasn't into it. Or hadn't been turned on to it recently. There's just no way to know.'

I nodded to acknowledge what he was telling me. 'What about the equipment? Did you see the broken quickdraw?'

'No. We heard afterwards that it was a quickdraw that failed. We've never heard of that happening before. The manufacturer asked if we could get hold of it because they want it back to see whether there was some kind of manufacturing fault or if it had been tampered with.'

'Really? These things just don't fail?'

Simon's eyes went as wide as saucers. 'Of course not. The whole industry is about making climbing safe for everyone. Safety records are what it is all about.'

I really needed to get hold of that bag of climbing evidence from the scene. I was still trying to establish if there was anything suspicious about his death. Well, beyond the fact that he appeared to be acting completely out of character. Getting the quickdraw inspected might tell me a lot.

'Can I bring it to you?' I asked. 'I expect to get hold of the evidence from the scene later today. The quickdraw will be with it. I also want to know why it failed.'

Now Simon and Maria looked like I was offering them a lifeline. 'Yes, please,' he gushed. 'Yes, if we can just prove the equipment had been tampered with...'

I took a moment to consider if I had any other questions, decided I didn't for now and said, 'Thank you for your time. We'll let you get back to your stock take now. I'll be in touch when I have the evidence.'

'We'll come to you, if that helps,' Simon offered. 'We are rather keen to see it, you see.'

I thanked them both, let Jermaine open the door for me and left them in their shop. I had a feeling of going around in a circle. Every bit of evidence, every question, just led me back to asking whether he had been murdered or not. Everything was ambiguous; he didn't climb alone, but he might have. He always used new equipment, but he might not have on that occasion.

The evidence that he was there alone was damning to the concept that he had been murdered, but I wasn't prepared to accept it as cast iron proof that there wasn't another person there. Not yet anyway.

Heading back to the car, my phone rang.

'Hello, Mike,' I answered the call with a smile.

'Good morning, Patricia. How goes the snooping and sneaking?'

Putting a hand to my chest in mock offense, not that he could see it, I said, 'I don't snoop and sneak, detective sergeant. I am a lady. I detect and investigate.'

He chuckled at the other end. 'Well, Lady Patricia, I have news for you. That bag of evidence from the Edward Foy investigation has already been returned to the wife. It was released this morning and she collected it an hour ago.'

At least I knew where I was going next.

'Okay, thanks for letting me know. Did you find out anything else?' Jermaine opened my car door and held it for me to get in, closing it behind me as I settled into my seat.

'With regard to the missing dog? No. So far as I am concerned, there is no gang of dog thieves operating in this area. No other cases reported. I think this is a lone incident.'

That pointed to the boyfriend yet again. I was trying to avoid jumping to a conclusion, but it felt right, and my instincts were generally on the money. I thanked Mike for letting me know and put my phone away.

From the passenger seat, Jermaine asked, 'How will you track down a man who appears to have no identity?'

I sucked on my teeth. It was a quandary. 'If it comes to it, we may need to lure the dognapper into a trap to catch them. Let's assume they are after the money. If they are not part of an organised gang, they will not have an elaborate method for collecting the money. I hope.'

He nodded, offering no comment. 'Where to next?'

'Back to see Mrs Foy. I want to examine Edward's climbing equipment.'

The journey took forty-five minutes, most of which was conducted on small B roads to take us from the small villages around the coast back to the motorway where I could finally open the throttle.

I didn't bother to call ahead; Mrs Foy had engaged me to investigate the circumstances of her husband's death and this was part of it. I expected her to still be off work as she was arranging the funeral this week though I ran a minor risk that she might not be at home.

There were two cars on the driveway when we pulled up. I felt it safe to assume one was hers – it was there this morning as well. However, parked behind it was a ten-year-old Renault Clio, a small hatchback with a pink princess sticker on the rear bumper that made me willing to bet it was her daughter Susie's car and that she was home too.

Perhaps she would be more willing to talk when face to face with me.

The door opened as I got to it, a young woman with a surly expression exiting the house. She wore denim shorts over black leggings and a loose-fitting hoody that covered her top half. Her hair was dyed black and she wore an abundance of black makeup. I wanted to believe the style was called Emo but couldn't be certain. Her ears had loops through them which distended the lobes to three or maybe four times their original size. It was not a look I would want to see on my daughter.

The black eye makeup just added to the surly look, but I wasn't about to be put off. Besides, she had on fluffy unicorn slippers that ended with a gold horn on the toes. How dangerous could she be?

'I asked you to leave my mum alone,' she snarled at me as she dumped the rubbish bag she was holding into the bin.

Jermaine moved in front of me to ensure no harm could come my way. It was an unnecessary move but one he would always make.

I levelled my eyes at her. 'Actually, Susie, you called me a rather unpleasant name and begged me to stop taking your mother's money. I'm afraid that is not how adults operate.' My dig at her age hit the mark, her brow creasing as the anger took hold. She was going to launch into a frenzy of fresh verbal abuse, but I got in first. 'Your stepfather was murdered. That's what your mother believes, and she asked me to determine if she is right or not. That is what I am going to do.'

Mercifully, before Susie could retort, her mother came to our rescue. 'Susie what are you doing?' she demanded while wearing a look of dismay.

Susie rounded on her. 'I can't believe you hired someone to prove it was murder. You're so stupid! He fell. It was an accident. Let it go!' Then she stormed back into the house, thumping up the stairs to leave a silent hole where she had been.

Sarah Foy looked embarrassed as well as tired and sad. 'I'm sorry,' she mumbled. 'Teenage girls.' She didn't need to say any more. I couldn't remember being the problem I hear so many parents complain about when their girls get to a certain age. But maybe I was and just don't recall it.

Invited inside, Jermaine closed the door behind us and followed me through to the living room when Sarah went that way herself.

'What can I do for you, Mrs Fisher?' she asked.

I could already see what I assumed was his climbing bag on the dining table in the next room. 'I believe you have had his gear returned to you this morning.'

'Yes, they called, and I went to collect it. I don't actually want it. It just seemed wrong to leave it there.'

'I would like to take it off your hands. It may contain vital evidence.'

She nodded. 'Of course. Please, take it. When you are done, you can throw it away or do whatever you want with it. I don't want it back.'

Susie appeared in the doorway still looking angry. 'You can't give it to her! I told you I want it.'

Sighing deeply, Sarah turned to her daughter. 'And I told you I don't want you climbing again. I couldn't...'

Susie snapped back at her, cutting off whatever she was going to say. 'You don't care about me! Don't care about what I want! I love climbing. It's not my fault Eddie fell.'

'No one's saying that,' Sarah tried to butt in.

Her daughter wasn't to be argued with though. 'I'm keeping his gear and I'm not stopping climbing.'

Sensing what might be coming, Jermaine had taken a careful pace backward and then moved behind Susie so that he was closer to the door and the bag of climbing gear. When she turned around to leave the room, he went first, collecting the bag, which was clearly heavy, and looping his arms through it, so it slid onto his back.

'Hey!' she yelled at him. 'Give that back!'

He ducked backward when she tried to grab for it, darting away as she came forward.

Sarah ran to intercept her. 'Susie, stop this. It isn't helping. I just want to know what happened to him. He wouldn't have gone up there alone. He just wouldn't.'

'You don't know that!' Susie screamed, holding her head as the tears began to fall. 'Don't let them take his things. They can't have them.'

Jermaine remained calm and quiet as the mother attempted to console the daughter but as Sarah tried to move in to hug her, Susie shoved her away, barging past her to get out of the room. 'You're going to ruin everything!'

I wasn't sure what Susie's parting comment meant; probably nothing, but Sarah was upset again, and I felt that she deserved to be left alone. Upstairs, a door slammed.

'Sarah, we'll let ourselves out. I'll be in contact as soon as I can tell you anything.' At the door, I thought of something else. 'Sarah, I need to know the name of the man Susie was with when Edward died.'

She nodded, accepting my request though she looked unhappy about it. 'Susie,' she called from the bottom of the stairs. 'Susie. I need to ask you something.' She got no reply but asked my question anyway. 'What was the name of the boy you were with last weekend?'

When she still got no answer and tried again, going up the first few steps and raising her voice, she got a tirade of abuse in return. Susie did not want to answer any questions or be helpful in any way. I decided there was nothing more to be gained at this time and that Sarah probably needed to be left in peace.

Once we were outside and the door was closed, I turned to Jermaine. 'We should head back to the house. I want to have a look at his equipment, and I want to see if we can find the boy Susie is supposed to have been with when her stepfather fell to his death.'

'You suspect her?' he asked.

A wry smile crept across my face as I channelled my inner Hercule Poirot. 'I suspect everyone, and I suspect no one.' I replied in what was probably a terrible French accent (French because who knows how to do a Belgian accent?).

Jermaine responded with a quizzical look; he had no idea who I had just impersonated. Not bothering to explain it, I said, 'I don't know. I thought her actions were strange, but it might just be how her grief is manifesting. She has an alibi and I doubt the police really questioned it because they had no cause to. Boys will lie for girls though; that much I know.'

'Very good, madam.'

Back at the house, Tom collected the car and took it back to the garage where he would most likely clean it both inside and out. Jermaine and I went inside, the heavy bag of climbing equipment still being carried by my butler.

'Where would you like it, madam?' he asked.

'Let's set up in the study. We need to find the boy Susie was with anyway.' Finding him would be impossible without a bit more information. All Sarah had been able to tell me was that his name might be Harry. A call to DS Mike Atwell was required.

As Jermaine hefted the bag on to the floor and began to unzip the various pockets and pouches, I made the call, getting Mike's familiar voice on the first ring.

'Patricia. Calling again so soon?'

'I need some more information. Would you like lunch?' I was going to invite him to the house where Mrs Ellis could rustle something tasty up for us, but he declined.

'Patricia it's nearly three o'clock,' he replied, making me look at the clock for the first time in hours. 'I had lunch more than two hours ago. I can't anyway, sorry. I have a genuine crime to investigate. There's been a spate of burglaries in King's Hill.'

'Oh, okay. I was hoping to get the name of the boy who provided an alibi for Susie Foy. She reported that she spent a night with someone, but she wouldn't tell me his name.'

He said, 'Give me five minutes,' and disconnected.

Behind me, Jermaine was laying out equipment and trying to match it to the inventory of new parts the Wessex's gave us. There were ropes, which were neatly looped and tied to stop them turning into a bag of snakes. Each rope was a different colour, my guess was each had a different purpose or that the colour indicated something. I could ask Barbie about it but doubted it was pertinent. The ropes took up most of the space in the bag but there were a lot of other items in there with them. Carabiners; one of the few things I did recognise, quickdraws which I could identify only because I learned about them yesterday, and myriad other items. Everything was in good order.

Except one broken quickdraw.

It still looked new though. Jermaine brought it over to the desk. 'I believe this is the item in question, madam.' It was in two parts, broken about the middle where the stitches on the material that linked the two carabiners had come undone. I picked it up to scrutinise where the material had separated. Obviously, I was no expert, but the thread used to stitch it together did not appear to have been cut, which would have suggested tampering. To my untrained eye, it just looked to have failed.

'Can you call Simon and Maria Wessex, please? Let them know we have the broken quickdraw and ask if they can come here to inspect it.'

'Very good, madam.' Jermaine walked a pace to make the call, so he wasn't crowding me. As he did that, my own phone rang, the screen displaying DS Atwell.

'Hi, Mike.'

'The name Susie Foy gave as an alibi is Harry White.' I wrote the name down on a pad I kept on the desk. 'He was interviewed at the time. I think Chief Inspector Quinn thought it was murder and was being thorough.

Harry got swept up before they changed their minds and called the investigation off. Are you getting anywhere?'

'I'm not sure,' I admitted. 'There is definitely something odd about Edward Foy's behaviour, but I don't know if that means he was murdered. Thanks for the name.'

'Oh, I have Harry's mobile number too,' he added as if just remembering. I wrote the number under his name as Mike recited it to me. 'I have to go. Let me know if you need anything else.' Then he was gone but I had a name and a number, so I called Harry next.

'Speak.'

That was all I got as a response to my call. I had never heard a person answer a phone like that in my life and it threw me for a second.

'Speak,' he demanded again. This time I got some words out but I had to rein in my desire to tell him off.

'Good afternoon. This is Patricia Fisher. I was hoping to ask...'

'No.'

'Excuse me?' I could feel my eyes narrowing as the insolent young man began to annoy me.

'No. I'm not going to answer any questions. Susie said you might call, trying to cause trouble. She told me to tell you to go fruit basket yourself with an apple.'

Obviously, fruit basket and apple were not the words he used, but I have no intention of repeating what he did say. I disconnected the call, quite certain there was no point in wasting any more time trying to speak to him.

69

Jermaine was hovering. 'Did I hear that young man being rude, madam?' Jermaine took such things quite personally.

'Yes. Susie got to him first. I shall have to come up with another way to find out what he knows.'

Jermaine nodded, then pointed to the computer I was sitting in front of. 'If I may, madam. I believe we can use some not-very-clever subterfuge to trick him into giving up what you want to know.'

Intrigued, I slid out of my chair. 'What are you going to do?'

Clicking the mouse to wake the computer, he began opening tabs. 'We know he is heterosexual, and that means he likes boobs. I just happen to have a friend who has some.'

'Hey, guys,' said Barbie, waltzing through the study door at exactly the right moment. 'What's going on?'

Jermaine said, 'We need to use you to draw in a young man who is unwilling to talk to Patricia.'

She was wearing yet another skin-hugging Lycra sports outfit. I know they were designed to be comfortable and eliminate bounce, but what they also did very efficiently was accentuate just how perfect her body was. Her chest appeared to defy gravity as only a twenty-two-year-old can achieve. I could assure her it would all be downhill from where she was, but she was bright enough to know that herself. The girdle of muscle keeping them in place would most likely fight the ravages of time for longer than most women, but the decline was inevitable. And it wasn't just her chest. Her waist was tiny and utterly flat, her midriff, when exposed, a taut wall of muscle but yet still soft and feminine unless she was engaged in a strenuous activity that would engorge the muscles to make them pop on the surface. Naturally blonde hair, eyes the colour of her native Californian sky, and a face, which could be at home on a glossy magazine, completed the look. She was a knockout. All we needed her to do was convince Harry White to meet her for a drink where she could wheedle from him every grain of truth.

'What does he look like?' she asked, crossing the room to check the computer screen. Harry looked like a boy barely out of his teens. He had a few residual spots from teenage acne, his hair was a mop on top of his head, and he looked a bit dirty, truth be told. Barbie said, 'No problem. Is he on a dating site anywhere?'

Jermaine smiled in response. 'That's just what I am looking into.'

Prancing effortlessly toward the door again, Barbie told us, 'I need a shower. Let me know if you can set something up for tonight, okay, and I'll dress accordingly.'

Jermaine had pictures of her on the computer already. This wasn't the first time she had been used as bait for a boy. Being drop-dead gorgeous wasn't her only talent, but it was one of the easiest ones to utilise and oh so effective. She paused on the way out of the door, crouching to look at the equipment.

'This is from the climber that fell?' she asked as she began to poke about.

I went over to see what she was looking at.

'There's no self-belay equipment here,' she told me as she continued to move things around. 'He would need at least a top and a bottom descender. There's nothing like that here. Of course, if he was truly free climbing, he wouldn't need them, but then he wouldn't need most of what he has here. He also wouldn't have been using a quickdraw. I saw the broken one on your desk.'

'So, what are you saying?' I asked, trying to get an exact answer.

She grabbed the bag and started checking the pouches and pockets. 'It doesn't add up.' Over her shoulder, she called. 'Jermaine, did you get everything out of the pack already?'

He was working at the computer, trying to find Harry on a dating site. 'I think so,' he murmured, more focused on what he was doing. 'Found him,' he announced, a tremor of jubilation sneaking into his ever-calm voice. 'He's on Meet Market.'

It was a dating site I had heard of at least. While Jermaine worked his magic, creating a fake profile for Barbie, she was rooting through the pack. She held it up and shook it. 'There's something in here somewhere. There're just so many little pockets to go through, I can't find it.' As a final resort she put the pack on the floor and used her hands to locate the article. 'Oh, this might be it. It's the right size and shape for a descender.'

Turning the pack over she found the zip that would finally reveal the last item in the pack, but it wasn't a piece of climbing equipment. It was a phone. She held it up to inspect it critically. 'This might have been in here for years.'

'Why do you say that?' I asked.

'Because it's such an old model.' She pressed the power button, but nothing happened. I knew very little about phones though I had learned to work my own well enough. Barbie frowned at it and turned it over to look at the base. Then she dug about in the bag again. 'It's dead,' she announced. 'It could just be the battery but there is no charger.'

'Can we plug it in somewhere?'

'Sure.' Barbie flicked her legs to propel herself off the floor, landing with both legs under her in some kind of ninja gymnastics move which would have broken both my hips had I tried it. 'I don't have anything that will fit this though. Jermaine, sweetie.' She took the old phone to show him. 'Have you got anything that would fit this?'

He squinted at where the power cable would go in. 'Yes.'

Oh good.

'When I was fourteen,' he added.

Oh. Not so good then.

Barbie took the phone and headed for the door. 'I'll see what I can get. They'll sell these online if no one here has anything that will fit. We'll have it tomorrow at the latest.'

With Barbie gone, I turned my attention back to Jermaine. 'How did you get on with the Wessex's?' I asked, spotting the broken quickdraw again.

'They are unable to attend directly but asked if we might host them tomorrow morning. Mr Wessex expressed a deep desire to see the item in person. He was keen enough to close his shop for the morning just to come here.

'Very good. We seem to have a busy schedule. I am going to take Anna for a walk. Good luck setting up Harry and Barbie.' I left him in the study to continue his work as I went in search of my dog. Anna probably didn't want to go for a walk; she was inherently lazy, but a trip to the post office would do her good. I had given Mavis plenty of time to work her magic but no number to contact me on. Emma hadn't called me either; how many hours would it take her to go through the footage? I decided not to call and check on her, guessing that she was most likely still at the post office with Mavis. I could kill two birds with one stone. I also remembered that I made a promise that Sam could see the puppies, so I ought to arrange that with his mum.

Poor Tom the handyman had probably only just finished cleaning the Aston and here I was about to take it out again.

The Magic of Mavis

I was right about Tom except that he was still cleaning it when I
arrived. Tom was in his sixties and had been at the house for decades
much like Mrs Ellis. As I understood it, he had very much a jack of all
trades which made him a great handyman. According to Jermaine, the
house had not been visited by a plumber, electrician, painter, decorator,
carpenter or other tradesman in more than twenty years all due to Tom's
ability to do anything a qualified person might. The one exception was gas
fitter, because one requires special permits to mess with the gas system.
There wasn't enough handyman work to keep Tom busy, but like any
industrious person, he found work for himself; gardening, cleaning and
helping out around the house with other tasks. Cleaning my cars was just
one of the many things he took on voluntarily. I think he liked to justify his
position.

'You really don't need to clean them every time I go out,' I assured him
as I came into the garage to find him scrubbing the wheels of my favourite
car.

'Oh, but I must, Mrs Fisher. It gives me pride to see them all gleaming.'
He saw me with my bag hooked over my left elbow and Anna being
restrained by my right hand as she pulled forward to sniff him. 'Sorry,
you're going out, aren't you? I should have been faster.'

Goodness, he was berating himself for not cleaning my almost spotless
car swiftly enough for me to go back out again.

'Please, Tom, there is no need to fret. I shall simply take another.' Then
I looked about the garage. I certainly had some cars to pick from.
Honestly, some of them terrified me. I could play it safe and take the Mini
Cooper, a little voice said in my head. Then the rather evil alter-ego

version of that voice spotted the Ferrari 360 spider in bright red and I knew which one I was going to drive.

Ten minutes later, after Tom had assisted me in manoeuvring the cars so I could get the Ferrari out, I was hurtling along the road to East Malling at twice the speed limit and ignoring the sensible voice telling me to slow down.

I did slow down, of course, long before I reached a bend or a bridle path from where a horse might suddenly emerge. It had taken only a single blip of the throttle to take the car from thirty to eighty miles per hour, a feat which it achieved in what felt like half a second. It certainly was exhilarating.

A tee junction forced me to slow and stop as I checked to make sure the road was clear. It wasn't. A large, new, silver Mercedes was sweeping down the road toward me. I let it pass but had to smile. Gawking at the car and then spotting me in the driver's seat, was none other than Angelica Howard-Box.

She saw it was me, that was for certain. I didn't have time to smile or wave before her car swept by, but I got to see her almost crash into a Rhododendron bush at the side of the road as she failed to pay enough attention to where she was going.

She didn't crash, thankfully, for she was the sort who would then find a way to blame me. I pulled out, turning across the road to head in the opposite direction. Anna looked up at me from the passenger seat, tilting her head to one side as if trying to ask a question. 'I'll walk you first, little girl. I promise.'

It wasn't far from my house to the post office; all of about two miles, which at the speed the Ferrari could do, didn't take long at all. I couldn't be taking risks like that again though, I chided myself. Any decent cop would have my licence off me in seconds.

Anna pulled excitedly at the lead again as we went into the woods. Her milk-filled breasts hung low beneath her already low underside. Grass, twigs, and other detritus didn't seem to bother her though as she bounded away through the underbrush the moment I unclipped her lead.

My phone rang in my pocket, the screen telling me it was my client Emma Maynard calling.

'Emma, hello. How are you getting on with the CCTV footage? Any luck?' I asked hopefully.

'Sorry. I went all the way through it but there was no sign of him ever going into the shop. That's not what I called for though.'

A gasp of excitement escaped my lips. 'Have they been in contact?'

'The dognappers? Yes. I got a message two minutes ago, so I called you right away. Can you come?'

I grimaced as I crouched and tried to spot Anna. She would come when I called. Eventually. Then I thought about what I needed to do about this development. Reaching a decision, I said, 'I can be there within the hour. What did the message say, please?'

There was a pause, probably the result of Emma taking the phone from her ear to switch between apps. 'They wrote, "I hope you have the ten thousand. You will need it for the exchange tomorrow. It will take place in Maidstone city centre. Be there at two o'clock and await further instructions. No police". That's it. That's the whole message. Should I get the money?'

I thought about that. It really wasn't my call. 'I think you have to do what you feel is right. If I haven't worked out who your boyfriend is by then, it might be the perfect opportunity to catch him. You don't need to call the police. I have several associates I can call on to help track him.' I thought of Jermaine and Barbie. She was fast and nimble, and he was part ninja part cat. 'It would be good to look like you have the money. If the dognapper is watching, I think we should assume he will be, then he will be looking to confirm you have it before he shows his hand. Chances are he will then take you somewhere else for the exchange.' I was running through all kinds of scenarios in my head. 'Listen, I'll be there in an hour or so. We can discuss strategy then.'

Once I was off the phone, I called for Anna. She popped out of the bushes looking excited just a couple of yards ahead of me, her tongue hanging out from all the fun she was having. Goodness knows what creatures she was finding to chase in the undergrowth, but I spoiled her fun by clipping her back to the lead.

'Sorry, little girl. Mummy has to go places and you get plenty of exercise chasing squirrels at home.' Despite that, we took a circuitous route back to the post office and that gave me time to call Jermaine.

'Madam.'

'Jermaine can you meet me with Barbie at Emma Maynard's house in a short while?'

'Of course, madam. Madam, I have been unable to secure a date for Barbie tonight. Harry White is not answering his dating app, but he has posted his intended location on social media, so I propose to go there with her this evening. Do you wish to remain home or accompany us?'

'Accompany you. Absolutely. Can you fit her with a wire?'

'I have already packed the gear and given Barbie a microphone, madam.'

I had purchased some listening equipment a couple of weeks ago when a case demanded it. It was multifunctional so could be attached to a person or to something static, great for putting under a table if you wanted to eavesdrop on a conversation. We tried it out in the kitchen to see if we could pick up what Mrs Ellis was doing. Mostly I was curious to see how good it was, but Jermaine and Barbie wanted to see how close it had to be to the person speaking in order for it to be effective.

Unfortunately, it was very effective, so when Tom came into the kitchen to interrupt Mrs Ellis's singing we discovered that the two of them were engaging in hanky-panky in their spare time, the sound of him smacking her bum and chasing her around the kitchen while she giggled something I might never forget. He had never married, and she was widowed, so there was nothing wrong in what they were doing, but I quickly turned the device off at our end before we heard any more. Then the three of us burst out laughing. What else could we do?

Nearing the post office, I estimated how long I would be, agreed to meet outside Emma's house, and ended the call.

Inside, the post office was deserted, just Mavis humming to herself in the back where the post office counter itself was located and Sharon, the sullen-looking teenager, on the till in the shop part.

Mavis spotted me approaching and perked up instantly. Before I got to the counter, she was beckoning for me to hurry up. 'You won't believe what I found out,' she blurted as soon as I was close enough for her to say it quietly yet still be heard.

79

I replied at normal volume. 'Please share your secrets.' I didn't think there was any need to whisper. No one was listening and I felt certain no one would care either.

Mavis continued to speak sotto voce. 'Your Charlie has hired himself a swanky divorce lawyer. I guess he thinks he should be entitled to some of that fortune you are sitting on now. The lawyer was in here earlier buying a paper.'

'It's not my fortune,' I pointed out. 'They are not my cars.' Although technically I thought they might be. As I understood it, the Maharaja had signed everything over to me. 'I don't have any more money than I ever did. It just looks like I have because I have been gifted a nice house to live in.'

Mavis wasn't to be put off though. 'Margery Reynolds recognised him from the TV, she said he dealt with the Duke of Essex's divorce that was all over the news last year. He got that model the Duke married more than two billion pounds and they were only married for six months.'

I had to admit that I didn't like the sound of what I was hearing but it wasn't what I came in for. 'Mavis, do you have anything to tell me about Emma Maynard and her gentleman caller?'

'Oh,' she said as if just remembering what she had agreed to do. 'Oh, yes. Emma came in and I let her go through the CCTV footage, but she couldn't find him. I was trying to watch too but the customers kept getting impatient.'

'Yes, I spoke to Emma already. It's disappointing. You were able to talk to villagers who live near her?'

'Well, I asked a lot of the people from her street, but no one remembered seeing a man going into her house. Except...'

I waited for her to continue her sentence, then had to prompt her. 'Mavis you were saying.'

'Well, now I think about it. When I asked Janice Porter; she lives directly opposite Emma's house, she started to say she had seen a man several times but not recently. But then her daughter Kara started arguing with her. Well, you know what teenagers are like. Kara said her mum shouldn't drink during the day because it makes her imagine things and that started a fight because Janice denied ever drinking during the day and it kind of went on for a bit and people in the queue got uppity because they were holding them up so Janice stormed off. I think it was Mrs Stanmore who did it, you know how cutting her tongue can be. Of course, I think young Kara might be right about her mum. She's been in here buying gin a few times since her Lionel walked out back at Christmas.'

I didn't know Janice Porter or her daughter Kara or about Janice's husband leaving. 'You say she lives opposite Emma? Do you happen to know the house number?' If she didn't, I would just knock on a door. I doubted I would get the wrong house more than once. She knew it though, the same way she seemed to know everything about everyone. She probably knew about Mrs Ellis and Tom the handyman.

Yet again, it wasn't much to go on. Who was I kidding? It was nothing to go on. It was about all I had though.

'So,' asked Mavis, 'what are you going to do about that divorce lawyer?'

I got to Emma's house earlier than expected; Barbie and Jermaine were yet to arrive, so I crossed the road to knock on Janice Porter's house. Approaching it, I could see the flickering light from a television playing inside her living room. It told me someone was in and I wasn't surprised when she answered the door a few moments later.

I smiled and tried not to look like a salesperson. 'Hello, Mrs Porter. I'm Patricia Fisher.'

'Yes, hello,' she replied, 'I know who you are. Mavis in the post office talks about you all of the time. Today she said she was helping you on a secret mission to find out who stole Emma's poor little doggy.'

It wasn't much of a secret mission if she was telling everyone about it, but I had to expect that from Mavis; she told everyone everything she knew at every opportunity.

'Yes, well I have been asked by Emma to see if I can find out what happened to her dog.' I deliberately left out that it had been dognapped and a ransom had been demanded.

'There was a ransom note wasn't there?' asked Janice, proving that any attempt at keeping Emma's business private was probably wasted the moment I spoke to Mavis.

Sighing I said, 'Yes. The most likely person to have taken the dog is a male friend she had coming to the house a while ago. Mavis at the post office suggested that you might have seen him.'

'Yes, I saw him. At least I think I did. He came by a few times. I can see Emma's front door from my couch, so I see when anyone goes to her door. Not that I spy on her,' she added quickly, realising she made herself sound like a nosy neighbour.

'Can you describe him for me?'

Her eyes lifted up and right as she scoured the memory portion of her brain. 'He was kind of average looking. He wasn't tall or muscular, or even particularly good looking. Emma could get someone much better, I guess that's what I am saying. He must have been at least a decade older than her, somewhere around forty but he still had all his hair. I can't stand bald men myself.'

Her description was almost exactly the same as the one Emma gave me. So now I knew that someone else had seen him but what did that give me? 'I don't suppose you saw him here on Saturday, did you? Emma's dog was taken some time not long before two o'clock.'

Again, she took a moment to search her memory. 'No, I don't think so. I haven't seen him in over a week, I think.'

'Did you happen to see his car ever?'

She shook her head firmly. 'No, I even looked once,' she admitted, then her cheeks coloured as she realised she just announced herself as the nosy neighbour she claimed to not be. 'Well, I was curious,' she tried to defend herself even though I had said nothing. 'I wondered what she saw in him and wanted to see if he drove a posh car which might mean he had money. I couldn't see anything though.'

'Were there any new cars in the street? Anything you didn't recognise as being one the neighbours owned?'

She shook her head again, not needing to think about her answer before giving it. 'I see the usual work vans, repair men, cable TV guys, postmen and gas men.' They are always about but those are the only ones I couldn't ever identify a definite owner for.'

This was a bust. Janice had seen the man I wanted to talk to, but she knew nothing more about him than I already did. He was a big, fat enigma.

I took a business card from my bag. 'If you remember anything else that might be pertinent to my enquiries, please call me.'

I thanked her, let her show me the door and went outside to find Jermaine and Barbie just pulling up. They were in the Mini Cooper. They could have taken any car but they, or perhaps Barbie, given the huge grin on her face behind the steering wheel, had chosen the nippy, nifty little hatchback over all the supercars and other prestige badges in the garage.

'Wow, Patty, this thing is so much fun!' she gushed getting out. 'I have to get myself one.'

I frowned and laughed as I shook my head. 'Barbie this one is yours. The cars in the garage belong to the house. You can take them and use them whenever you want. They are not mine, despite what the Maharaja says.'

'Okay, Patty,' she replied mockingly. 'They really are yours though, aren't they?'

Technically, they probably were. 'Nevertheless, you are to choose and use whichever one you wish whenever you wish. That goes for you too, Jermaine. I don't want to see you walking to the dry cleaners in West Malling; take the Bentley.' He opened his mouth and I knew he was going to protest. 'It's what John Steed would drive,' I pointed out.

A grin stole across his face. 'Actually, he did drive a Bentley. He also had a saucy little AC Greyhound Coupe.'

'Well, we don't have one of those,' I replied. Then had to question my statement. 'Do we?' There were so many cars in the garage I genuinely wasn't sure what we had.

With a small chuckle, Jermaine said, 'No, madam, we do not.'

I indicated toward Emma's house. 'Shall we?'

I guess Emma had seen us coming again because she opened the door before we got to it. She was expecting me of course.

'Hi, I'm Barbie,' said Barbie, getting there first and extending her hand.

Emma looked surprised but managed to say, 'Um, okay.' Like a lot of people, she was thrown by Barbie genuinely looking like a barbie doll.

Inside her house, Emma got straight down to business, whipping out her phone to show us all the message. 'I just want my dog back,' she told us before we could crowd around and read it. 'I contacted the bank this morning to arrange to withdraw the money. I don't have quite that much so I had to borrow some, but I would rather pay it and get Horace back than spend the rest of my life knowing I chose money over him. It just seems... callous.'

I understood her point of view. I would pay anything to get Anna back if someone took her. 'Let's hope you don't have to choose. We know where you have to be and when. Barbie, Jermaine, and I will be positioned out of sight but within easy reaching distance of you. We will be filming the event from multiple angles and will be back here tomorrow morning to fit you with a wire so we can record anything that is said.'

Barbie gave her an encouraging look. 'Patty isn't a famous sleuth for no reason. She's really good. We'll get your little dog back if we can.'

'And catch the person behind this,' added Jermaine, his voice sounding utterly confident.

Emma bit her lip to stop herself from sobbing; she badly wanted Horace back. Keeping her money and catching the dognapper were entirely secondary.

Touching her arm to impart my empathy, I got down to the detail of what we were going to do and how it would all happen.

We were going to get this guy.

A Date with Harry

I felt a little out of place going into a bar filled with students and young people. I could have stayed home. Jermaine and Barbie didn't need me, and I was here only because I felt invested and would feel more out of place sitting at home while they were out working.

They both volunteered for the task, Jermaine seeing it as his duty and Barbie feeling that she had to pay me back for giving her and Hideki a grand place to live for free. Regardless of their thoughts on the matter, I was still paying them even though they insisted I shouldn't. The investigation business made money; they were part of that so they got paid, and I wouldn't discuss it.

Barbie's boyfriend, Hideki, came along as well. Enjoying an evening off from the long hours at the hospital, he planned to spend it with Barbie. This probably wasn't what his plan entailed but he offered no argument when she gleefully announced she was the bait in a sting operation. He looked casual, yet smart, in a dark blue silk shirt and tight-fitting trousers. His figure was athletic and lean, his eyes sharp and his smile never more ready than when Barbie was in his company. The two of them seemed very much in love.

Barbie slipped her hand out of his as we neared the bar; she was supposed to be single and available. She started drawing attention the moment she walked through the door. At twenty-two, she was a little older than the average in the establishment, but only just and it wasn't like she wore a label claiming her age. For tonight's escapade, she chose a bright red cat suit with a plunging neckline, running shoes which somehow matched her outfit and a black Wonderbra which was doing... well, wonders for her ample chest.

Young men were staring, and they were not staring at her face. Jermaine was at her side, but he wore a rainbow pin in his lapel in case there was any question about his sexuality. I trailed behind like an old woman chaperoning her kids as Hideki came through the door and turned left, splitting off so the four of us wouldn't look like we were together.

Barbie whispered, the microphone in her hair picking up her words, 'Let me know if you spot him. I'll be at the bar getting drinks.'

Instantly thirsty, I replied, 'I'll have a...'

'Gin and tonic,' she finished my sentence with a chuckle, heading for the bar as the crowd parted like the Red Sea. I tried to follow her but found the Red Sea had closed again behind her as young men found the tight cat suit gave them plenty to look at from behind as well.

I gave up and found a table, settling onto a high stool from which I could scan around the room. I had Harry's picture on my phone, but I couldn't see him anywhere.

'They don't have any gin, Patty.' Barbie's voice arrived in my ear via the microphone and speaker system we had set up. Jermaine and Hideki had earpieces too so the four of us could chat to each other at a normal, or even whispered, volume without anyone else knowing.

Sighing as I took in the sign above the bar offering student drinks at bargain prices, I settled on a sparkling water.

'He just walked in,' said Jermaine, his voice drawing my eye to the door as a gaggle of boys entered.

At the bar, Barbie passed my drink to Jermaine and lifted the straw of her own to her bright red lips, sauntering back through the crowd with her hips swaying and looking sexy as all hell. The crowd parted once more to let her through.

She made a beeline for Harry, the boys coming through the door freezing as they saw her advancing in their direction. Harry had a far better-looking friend with him, who seized his opportunity to hit her with a suave smile and a cool pick up line I didn't catch. Whatever it was didn't work because she blanked him completely, grabbed a fistful of Harry's shirt and dragged him behind her as she headed back through the bar to find a secluded corner. She didn't even bother speaking.

Harry looked bewildered but he wasn't fighting it.

Barbie's voice came through our earpieces. 'Hello, Harry. My name's Barbie. I'm new in town and very lonely. Will you be my friend tonight?' She was pushing the sultriness up to level eleven, her voice coming out in a slutty whisper that must have been going directly to his trousers. I glanced at Hideki, finding him through a gap in the crowd, but his face wasn't betraying any emotion.

Harry managed to say, 'Um,' his voice coming out as a desperate squeak as if it hadn't broken properly yet.

'Take your time, lover,' she purred, 'After all, we've got all night.'

I heard him gasp, a sort of excited yet terrified noise which escaped his lips whether he wanted it to or not. He cleared his throat and tried again. 'Um, you're not from around here?'

She giggled as if a little tipsy. 'No, sweetie, I'm from California. Would you like to see my tan lines?'

He almost choked this time.

Barbie knew what she was here for; we needed to know if he had really been with Susie last weekend or not. She was going about it a different way to the method I might have used, but then I wasn't sure what I might have done to get him to talk and couldn't have taken the approach she was employing if I wanted to.

As the crowd moved, I got a look at them across the room. They were squeezed into a booth with Barbie sitting almost on top of him. Her right hand was on his thigh and she was leaning forward so he could see down her top. He looked utterly mesmerised.

'I'm going to want to get out of here shortly, Harry. I want you to get me turned on before we leave though. Why don't you tell me all about your most recent conquest? Tell me all about what you did to her, how you left her breathless. Will you do that for me?'

I swear I heard him swallow, his nerves visible even from here.

She had to cajole him a little more, but he licked his lips a few times and finally started talking. 'Well, I'm not really one to kiss and tell...'

'You can tell me, big boy,' she purred in his ear.

I glanced at Hideki again. He didn't look as calm and cool as he had before. In fact, he was beginning to look a little agitated. Listening to his girlfriend snuggling up to another man wasn't something he enjoyed.

My attention was drawn back to Barbie and Harry as he started talking. Giving in to her cajoling, he finally had a dirty story for her. 'Okay, well, just last weekend, I invited a girl over to my digs at the Uni. We were going to watch the new Star Trek series, the one with Jean Luc Picard returning.' He saw her look and realised he was drifting off topic. 'So, anyway, she turned up with two of her friends, so there was me and three girls squeezed into my little room. And, and, one of them had brought a jar of caramel sauce with her and they all wanted to lick it off my…'

He was clearly making it up as he went along, imagining a ridiculous ménage that was unlikely to ever happen to anyone anywhere unless they worked in the adult film industry. Maybe that was it and the dirty little monkey had been watching porn.

Barbie put a finger to his lips to silence him. 'Tell me about Susie, Harry. Tell me all about how you pleasured her.'

His face screwed up on itself in confusion. 'Hold on. How do you know about Susie? How do you know my name even? I have never seen you before, and trust me when I say I would remember, but you knew who I was the moment I walked in.' Now he was looking around the room for his mates. 'Is this a wind up? Have those tossers paid you to do this? Are they recording me making a prat of myself?'

He was getting upset and beginning to get up. The gig was a bust, Barbie overplaying her hand. We would have to confront him directly and convince him it was in his best interest to tell us exactly what did happen last weekend.

Barbie wasn't beaten yet though. As he got up, she grabbed one of his hands and placed it on her left boob. 'Does that feel like a wind up?' she asked.

I saw Hideki tense.

Harry paused, halfway to upright but clearly no longer wanting to leave. 'Um, no,' he admitted.

'I'm a friend of Susie's. I'm an exchange student and I just got here a few weeks ago. We are on the same courses at Uni. She told me about the great... what was the word she used? Oh, yes. Great shag. She said you were a great shag and I... well,' she was being coy now. 'A girl has needs.'

He sat back down, utterly hooked. His hand was still cupping her boob, but she looped her fingers between his and held his hand to end the public fondling.

Jermaine had worked his way around the room to get closer to Barbie's Japanese boyfriend, but Hideki was keeping himself under control. He might not like watching Barbie in action, but she was playing a role and he wasn't going to interrupt her.

Barbie's voice was back in my ear, 'Shall we try again?' she asked. 'Why don't you tell me about Susie?'

'Um,'

'Yes?'

'Um, well. I don't really remember all that much about it.'

Barbie smiled sweetly. 'But she said you were amazing. You must remember something. Did you meet her in here?'

'No,' he replied. 'Over the road,' he nodded with his head to a place on the other side of the street. 'She just came up to me and wanted to dance and then we were kissing, and she wanted to go back to my place.'

'Did you know her already?'

'No. It was a bit like tonight really. She just walked up to me and laid it out on a plate.'

'But you don't really remember it?'

'Not after the bar. I had already had quite a few to drink. I think I might have passed out when we got back but I woke up naked and in bed with her and she was naked too. We were both pretty wasted.' He pursed his lips and frowned, then leaned away from Barbie to get a better look at her. 'You're not here to pick me up at all, are you? Are you a cop?' he asked before she could answer the first question.

Barbie gave him a wry smile. This time the gig really was up. 'No, Harry, I am not a cop.'

'But you are investigating Susie's dad's death, aren't you? She asked me to look out for an old lady called Patricia Fisher.'

Old lady?

'Susie says she is snooping around and conning money out of her mum by making her think her dad might have been murdered.' Barbie didn't bother to correct him about the dad/stepdad thing; it would be unnecessarily pedantic. 'You're not her, but... what? You work for her?'

I was already crossing the room; we had heard enough, and it was time to rescue Barbie. She saw me coming, waving to me as I got close.

'This is the old lady?' asked Harry.

'I'm fifty-three,' I protested though gritted teeth.

Harry just looked confused. 'Yeah, that's what I said.'

Making eye contact with Barbie, I said, 'I think we should head for home.'

She patted Harry's hand and got up. 'Can I have your number?' he called after her, hopeless hope in his face.

93

She did her best to keep her expression neutral as she replied, 'No, Harry. I have a boyfriend. I'm sorry for the subterfuge.'

Looking sad but stoical, Harry nodded at the reply he expected. 'That's okay. I got to feel your boobs. That should help me finish my box of Kleenex tonight.'

Barbie and I both said, 'Ewwww,' as our faces screwed up in disgust.

Hurrying away, Barbie said, 'Teenage boys are so icky.'

At the door, Hideki caught up with us. Barbie asked, 'Everything alright, babe?'

'Um, yes,' he lied.

She smiled at him as she took his hand, leaning in to whisper something that made his eyes dilate. I left them to it, looking around for my tall, Jamaican butler. 'Anyone seen Jermaine,' I asked, standing on my toes to see over the crowd.

Hideki answered. 'I, ah. I think he met someone.' I raised my eyebrows. 'He was chatting with a man at the bar the last time I saw him.' I hadn't paid him much attention, far too focused on Barbie and Harry to worry about the tallest, most dangerous man in the room. Jermaine appeared the next moment, fighting his way through the crowd to get to us at the doors.

Looking a little guilty, though there was no reason for it so far as I was concerned, he said, 'My apologies, madam. I was... waylaid.'

'Jolly good. Shall we go home now?' I asked.

Barbie giggled at something Hideki had just said to her and danced away from him. 'Sure,' she said. 'I have some surplus energy to burn off.'

Another Case

It was only when I got home and had my shoes off and my feet up that I remembered I was supposed to knock at Melissa's house to arrange Sam's puppy visit. I had intended to call her but discovered I lost her number when I dropped my phone in the upper deck pool on the Aurelia. It was too late in the evening now for me to find a number and make a call so I would have to try again tomorrow. There would probably be time in the morning between other tasks. I also remembered what Mavis said about Charlie getting a lawyer.

I had to wonder about that. Since the incident with Emily at his house, we had spoken only once. I was divorcing him, so it was all on me to make the arrangements and it should have been a simple enough business, or would have been if I hadn't found out about the money Charlie had been keeping from me for our entire marriage. No sooner had I found out about that than I was gifted a house and cars and everything else I could ever ask for, the Maharaja of Zangrabar choosing to be incredibly generous just because I rescued him, saved his life and prevented his throne from falling into the hands of a scheming uncle. I knew what he had given me was a drop in the ocean for one of the richest men on the planet, but it was still a lot for me.

However, it changed my attitude toward Charlie and what he had. I no longer felt inclined to take half of our shared assets, not that I discussed it with anyone, and felt certain everyone would tell me I was crazy to let him off the hook when he had behaved so badly. It just didn't seem worth the effort to me.

Then I failed to do anything about the divorce; my new business and mounting cases demanding my attention be focused elsewhere. Now though, if I discovered he was gunning for me and thinking he could grab a share of what the Maharaja had so generously given, then I was going to get a lawyer of my own. Two lawyers. Heck, I might even get a team.

I was alone in my three-room master suite. Barbie had taken Hideki to their room. The sight of her being fondled by another man, albeit, a scruffy teenager, had got him all hot and bothered which I think she was planning to use to her advantage. Jermaine had tried to continue working, offering to draw me a bath and bring me a drink. I sent him away; he deserved to relax as much as anyone else. He needed to meet someone and have some kind of a life outside of looking after me. Being my butler somehow filled him with purpose and joy, but he had to want more from life. I wondered if anything would become of whoever he was talking to in the student bar earlier.

Anyway, he had grumpily agreed and headed to his own rooms, though he was good enough to carry the puppies and their bed upstairs as I carried Anna. They were all on my bed now, the little puppies playing rough and tumble, nipping at each other and making little excited barking noises as they wagged their tiny tails.

I thought about calling Charlie, but it really was late, and I didn't feel like fighting now. What I did do was power up my laptop and check my emails. The business is advertised in several local magazines or papers, both in print and online and Jermaine did some clever internet stuff that meant my business would pop up as a search result if people used certain key words. I really didn't understand it, but it had increased the amount of communication zipping back and forth.

Jermaine suggested it might be worth hiring someone to sift them if I didn't want to do it myself. He was probably right, but I hadn't looked into that yet and wasn't sure it was truly necessary.

Opening the business mail inbox, I found, to no great surprise, that Jermaine had already read and sorted them, marking some for my attention and undoubtedly committing those unworthy of my attention to the recycle bin.

There were seven for me to read. The first asked for help with a missing cat, the second claimed they were the victim of internet harassment. However, it was the third that got my attention. The email came from Jerry Brock. His daughter and son-in-law had gone missing from their home a week ago. They hadn't replied to any messages since, their car was still on the drive, and neither had let their work know they would be absent. In his words; they had just disappeared. The police were investigating, but I knew they couldn't put much resource to what might prove to be a spontaneous week away in Benidorm.

Despite the hour, I called the number he gave on his email.

A man's voice answered the phone, 'Good evening. Jerry Brock.' He sounded like someone who answered the phone a lot in whatever he did for a living and had developed brevity.

I was rereading his email when I said, 'Hello. This is Patricia Fisher. You contacted me about your missing daughter and son in law.'

'Yes! Yes, goodness, I'm so glad you called. That was fast. I only sent the email an hour ago.' I looked at the received time; he was right.

'Well, I like to stay on top of things, and this sounds like a time-sensitive case.' Okay, I was making it up a bit and the time-sensitive thing was that they might just turn up before I got any billable hours in if I didn't act fast. To me, the most likely scenario was that the couple had decided to do something spontaneous, switched off their phones and gone with it. I even hoped that was the case because it would be better than finding a body or bodies. I wanted to have a new case to look into though because I was getting nowhere with Emma's missing dog, Horace, and Sarah's murdered, or not, husband. Soon, I would just run out of ideas for the cases and would then need billable hours elsewhere.

Jerry was buzzing with excitement. 'Oh, it is time-sensitive, it really is. How soon can you start?'

I knew what answer the client expected to hear. 'Right away, Mr Brock. In fact, I am at my laptop now starting to perform some research. I will need to meet you. I have a contract for you to sign, I need to take a deposit from you, and I expect to have a lot of questions to ask. Can we meet tomorrow?'

'Absolutely, Mrs Fisher. Just tell me when and where.' He really was keen. It presented me with an opportunity though. I hadn't really used the office in Rochester since I rented and furnished it. All my client meetings, the primary purpose I envisaged for it, were conducted at their homes. It would be nice to go there for a change.

I set the meeting up for five o'clock the next afternoon, thanked him for his business even as he was gushing with gratitude that I had taken the case, and ended the call.

It was close to bedtime, but I felt invigorated. There was a new case for me to consider and a blank sheet because I knew nothing at all at this point. Maybe they were in a cottage in Dorset, snuggled up in bed rekindling their marriage. Maybe they had been kidnapped by the Mafia. It spoke volumes about my past that I considered the latter just as likely.

Grabbing a fresh A4 notepad and a pen, I arranged my pillows to make myself comfortable and started looking into their lives.

Wednesday Morning

Breakfast the following morning was all about the ransom exchange and what we could do to make sure we got the result we wanted. Barbie had a class at nine o'clock so had to dash but would be back after lunch, taking a half day so she could be involved.

We saw Hideki briefly when we returned from our morning jog. He looked tired, his junior doctor's shift rotation demanding a lot from him and he was heading back to London now to start the next rotation.

The ransom exchange was as planned as we could make it. We knew where we were going to be and where Emma would be. I was going over to her place again later with Jermaine to fit her with a wire and make sure she wasn't too nervous. I wanted her to believe she was safe and that we would be with her no matter where the dognapper might ask her to go. Jermaine provided a map of the town centre from the internet, zooming in to capture the part we needed. On it we marked where each of us would be and discussed what we might do in different circumstances – like, for example, the dognapper being brazen enough to turn up in person.

In that event, Jermaine was going to collar him while I called the police. With or without the dog in his possession, the game was up the moment we recorded him asking for the money. It was another thing to go through with Emma, as I wanted her to understand what we needed to hear him say for an easy conviction.

With the planning done, Barbie had to dash, and I had an errand to run so I was going to walk Anna shortly. Before I could get to that, the doorbell rang, and Jermaine began his slow walk to answer the front door.

I stayed where I was, waiting for the echoing of voices as Jermaine led our visitors back through the house. The Wessex's were expected so it was no surprise when they came into my home office being led by my butler.

'Good morning,' I smiled at them,

Marie was taking things in her stride, but Simon was thrown by the size and grandeur of the house. Like other people coming here for the first time, me included, his eyes were darting about as he tried to take everything in. I brought his attention back by crossing the room with my hand extended.

'Hello again,' said Marie, nudging her husband with an elbow to get him to focus.

'Yes, sorry, yes, hello,' he managed.

'The quickdraw,' I announced as I took it from the desk to show to them.

That brought him back to the here and now. With the item in his hands, he was able to scrutinise it, turning it this way and that as Marie watched. As he held it up to the light, she said, 'We contacted the manufacturer already. They will send a person if we report that there is something to see. They take this type of thing very seriously. If they suspect it has genuinely failed, they will be all over it. But if they think someone might have tampered with it, their effort will double as they go all out to maintain their safety record.'

I guess that made sense.

Simon's brow was creased with concentration. 'I think this has been fiddled with. I just can't tell for certain. They're going to have to send someone.'

'How long will that take?' I asked.

Finally, he stopped staring at the broken halves of the quickdraw and looked at me. 'I got the impression they would come straight away. I think they will be here tomorrow if I call them shortly.'

I nodded; I liked that. A definitive answer on the quickdraw by an expert would help.

'Can we take it?' asked Marie.

'Of course, please do. Please let us know if they are sending someone and when they will arrive. I am keen to hear what they have to say.'

Simon promised he would do exactly that and the couple departed, Jermaine escorting them back to the front of the house so they didn't get lost. I went to look for my dog.

Anna and her puppies were all sleeping when I found them in the pantry. The sound of the door opening made all five heads rise as they looked to see who might be coming in. Little Georgie, the only girl in the litter, flopped out of the basket and ran over to me, her clumsy puppy legs defying her instructions, so she spilled on the floor. Falling over couldn't quell her excitement. She bounced back up and started running again, her unbridled joy demanding I crouch to snag her from the floor when she reached my hands.

There are few things in the world that smell as good as a warm puppy. Not that I think I could bottle it as a new perfume but as she snuggled on my chest and tried to bite my chin with her tiny, needle-like puppy teeth, I cherished it. I couldn't stop myself from cooing at her, making baby talk as she waved her paws in the air.

'Have you decided what you are going to do with them, Mrs Fisher?' asked Mrs Ellis, appearing in the pantry doorway.

I opened my mouth to talk, which earned me a lick to my upper teeth as Georgie lunged to show her affection. After wiping my face, I replied, 'Not yet. I don't think keeping them is a good idea. I need to make sure they go to good homes though.'

Mrs Ellis had a healthy glow to her face which, given that it was only just after nine o'clock, probably wasn't from the sherry. There was mud on her hands, I noticed, so she had most likely just come in from outside, where it was a little nippy this morning. She saw me looking at her hands and said, 'Pulling up carrots. Miss Berkeley requested a carrot soup for lunch.' That sounded likely. 'Will you advertise them?' she asked.

I looked down at Georgie again. I had never owned a puppy before. They were utterly delightful but of course they do not remain puppies for very long. Anna had been fully grown when she came to me, the unwanted possession of a Japanese crime lord. I didn't know how old she was or when her birthday occurred. To get around the latter, we would celebrate the day she was handed to me.

Keeping the puppies was a bad idea, but I wasn't sure I could let go of them either. 'I think I will worry about that later, Pam.'

Discussing them gave me an idea though. I popped Georgie back in the basket with her brothers, Paul, John, and Ringo and picked up Anna instead. 'Are you getting lazier, little girl? Or are these puppies keeping you up all night?' She didn't answer, but she also didn't seem very keen to go for a walk. Which was precisely what we did next.

Melissa Chalk lived a little more than a mile from me now that I had moved to what I might always think of as the Maharaja's house. It would be a pleasant walk each way and would take between ten and twenty minutes depending how distracting Anna found the local smells, scent marks, and critters living in the bushes.

I knew Melissa didn't work. She hadn't done since Sam left school and needed to have mum at home full time. I think they did okay financially because her husband, Paul, had a good job that provided more than enough for them both. Not having a job didn't mean she would be at home, but I was hedging my bets because Anna needed to be exercised.

It paid off, Melissa opening the door and looking surprised but pleased to see me. 'Sam told me he saw you at the post office. I wasn't sure whether to believe him or not; you know what his imagination is like.'

'No, he had it right. It was lovely to see him.' He appeared in the hallway behind her, a DVD box in his hands. 'Hi, Sam,' I waved.

'Hi, Mrs Fisher,' he waved back, dropping the DVD box so the shiny silver disc popped free and rolled away. He chased after it.

'Come in, won't you?' urged Melissa, stepping back from the door as she beckoned me in. 'I feel like I haven't seen you in months.' Then she sniggered at herself – her comment was a joke. Everyone knew about my around the world cruise; it had become not just public knowledge but a global news event on a couple of occasions. We shared a smile.

'Do you fancy a cup of tea?' she asked. 'I was just going to put the kettle on.'

'Sounds lovely.'

I followed her through the house, her eyes glancing down at Anna as she trotted happily toward the kitchen. Her brow was knitting together as she tried to work something out. 'Did you have a dog before you went away?'

'No.' I smiled. 'I picked her up in Japan. It was one of those odd moments in life when something happens, and you just have to go with it. She's one of the reasons I popped in today actually.' Busily filling the kettle, Melissa paused to look at me. 'She had puppies,' I explained. 'I promised Sam he could see them but didn't think to check with you first.'

'Oh, riiiight. That make sense. He has been going on about a puppy he knows for days now.'

Overhearing his mother, Sam appeared again. 'Yeah, I know a puppy. I see it when...'

Melissa flapped her arms at him to shoo him from the kitchen. 'I thought you wanted to watch that film?'

Forgetting the dog and remembering the film in his hands, a beaming smile split his face. 'Yeah! I love this film.' He twirled about on the spot and dashed away.

Automatically, I said, 'Bless him. He's such a sweet boy.'

Melissa sighed. 'But he's not a boy. He's thirty-one next April. I should be thinking about grand kids.' She caught herself wallowing just as the kettle clicked off. 'Listen to me moaning. At least I got to have a child.' We only ever talked about my miscarriage the once, she bumped into me a few days after it happened, and the bump was yet to go down, so she asked me about how my baby was doing and if it was kicking yet. She couldn't have known. It was my first miscarriage. The first of many.

105

Raising Sam, I think there were times when she thought I was the lucky one. Thankfully, she never said it.

To move the conversation on, I said, 'I assume it's okay for him to come to see the puppies then?'

She handed me my mug of tea. 'Of course, Patricia. I'll bring him over whenever you like. It will be nice to get out of the house. And, of course, I am curious to see that mansion you are living in now.'

My cheeks tried to colour which I hid by taking a slurp of tea. It was far too hot, scalding my mouth so I had to spit it back into the mug. Melissa's eyes were wide as she stared at me. I was such a klutz.

'Sorry,' I manged with a drip of tea hanging off the end of my nose.

'Are you embarrassed to talk about it?' Melissa asked, clearly seeing my reaction for what it was.

'God, yes. It's too much. I have a butler. I have a cook. I have three Ferraris.'

'You can give me one,' she joked.

'I feel like such a fraud. I didn't do anything to deserve it.'

Melissa frowned at me over the top of her mug as she blew on the surface to cool it. 'I don't think anyone else sees it like that. Especially that Maharaja friend of yours.'

We talked for a while and drank our tea. Melissa demanded I tell her all about the cruise and all the amazing places I had been. I left out most of the shooting and explosions in my retelling but not all of them as some gave context. She agreed to bring Sam over the following morning at nine and mostly, it was just nice to catch up. I had been home for more than a month but starting the business and the flurry of activity that caused plus the new house and all the excitement that went with it meant I was close to being a recluse so far as the other villagers were concerned.

Anna snuffled around the kitchen and poked her nose into gaps she thought might yield food but had given up long before I announced it was time to leave. I had to get ready to catch the dognapper, praying I might close one of my cases.

I could see Emma but doubted she could see me. I was inside WH Smith, standing by the magazines where I could look over the top of a stand facing the street and see her through the window. In three strides, I could be out the door.

Emma was at the top of Fremlin Walk, a pedestrianised area of Maidstone where all the shops and restaurants converged. There were four different streets peeling off from it. Or four different ways to go might be a better way of looking at it. We were confident the dognapper didn't know any of us, so we were not in disguise, but we were keeping out of sight.

Jermaine had taken himself to a coffee shop on the corner of two streets where he was pretending to play with his phone while keeping an eye on Emma. Barbie, dressed in sports gear and ready to chase our dognapper down if he showed himself, was hovering near a florist. Between the three of us, we had our bases covered.

Emma looked nervous, waiting around with a handbag full of money for the next message to ping into her phone. She checked it continually, refreshing the screen to see if the message had somehow appeared but not triggered the new message chime.

Two o'clock had been and gone. It was nearly quarter past now and there was still no message. Emma looked my way, then down at her feet as she said, 'I don't understand. Why bring me here if they are not going to show?'

The microphone in her top picked up her voice so all three of us heard her.

I spoke next, 'Has anyone seen anyone who looks suspicious?' We all had a description for her boyfriend just in case he was the culprit, but brown hair, medium build, average height, somewhere around forty years old yielded far too many targets.

'Nothing, madam,' replied Jermaine.

Barbie said, 'Same here.'

Huffing in disappointment, I addressed Emma, 'Emma I don't suppose you have seen your former boyfriend, have you?'

'I'm afraid not. You'll know if I do though because I'll be screaming at him and beating him to death with my handbag.' She sounded angry and also disappointed. She wanted her little dog back more than anything and this was a total bust.

'Let's give it another five minutes, okay?' I suggested to a round of bored agreement. We had approached the task with excitement, each of us genuinely believing we could catch the dognapper today. We had been waiting for an hour already, having arrived before Emma to get in place.

It was my expectation that she would be messaged with an instruction to go somewhere else, being led from point to point until the dognapper was content she wasn't being followed, which she would be; the three of us switching around to tail her. It was that, or the dognapper would brazenly walk up to her, believing his size and strength would intimidate her and he could just make off with the money.

Had that happened, Jermaine would have deftly put him on his butt and kept him there while we waited for the police. While I was running all this through my head for the hundredth time, a whole lot of nothing else was happening.

But then it did.

Jermaine had just enough time to say, 'I believe I have spotted someone watching Miss Maynard.' He didn't have time to react though.

I was watching her through the window, so I saw it when a male figure in jeans and a hooded top darted in close to her as he walked by. He snatched her handbag and started running.

It happened so fast he got the drop on everyone. Whether deliberate or through serendipity, he had chosen to run along Week Street heading toward the station which placed Barbie and me behind him. By the time we saw what was happening, he already had a forty-yard lead and was running flat out. Only Jermaine could hope to stop him but a gaggle of mothers with pushchairs blocked Jermaine's intercepting path and allowed the runner to get through.

Barbie, who started further away from the runner than me, shot by me as if I was standing still. I wasn't, I was running flat out, but I had on calf-length boots and autumn clothes, plus I'm not a twenty-two-year-old gym bunny genetically spliced with a gazelle.

I was drawing a lot of stares as I ran along the street. So were Barbie and Jermaine who were both disappearing into the distance as I failed to keep pace. Jermaine bellowed, 'Stop that man!' as he gave chase, but the good people of Maidstone were not of a mind to intercept anyone by throwing themselves in his path.

The runner in the hoody was getting away, reaching the end of Week Street and streaking past the train station as he crossed the road. He was about to pass the prison, located in the heart of Maidstone town centre, but after that he would enter the labyrinth of side streets and alleyways and vanish.

Not even Barbie, who had left Jermaine in her wake, would be able to catch him before he escaped. Once he got to the rows of terrace houses that border the city centre, he was as good as gone and Emma's money would be gone with him.

Was he just a bag snatcher? Was he the dognapper or did he work for him?

I was out of breath having run a hundred yards already, drawing in great gulping lungfuls as I slowed my pace. I wasn't achieving anything by continuing to chase and in my ear, I could hear Emma crying and wailing. There were people back on Fremlin Walk trying to comfort her after seeing the theft, but they couldn't know what it meant.

I could still see the distant figure of the bag snatcher. He was more than two hundred yards ahead of me now and still running for all he was worth. In just a few more seconds he was going to be around the side of the prison and would vanish from sight.

He needed to dodge a short, round black woman as she got in his way, but to my surprise, as he jinked to the left to avoid her, she stuck out a stiff arm and damned near took his head off.

He ran into her arm with his face, which stopped instantly while the rest of his body continued forward. The net result saw his feet fly into the air as he inverted and crashed to earth on his skull. I don't know if he was able to get up and keep going because he never got the chance.

Barbie wasn't that far behind him and running flat out so once he stopped moving, she closed the distance fast, but if she intended to apprehend him, she didn't get the chance either.

Breathlessly, I performed a mental fist pump but started running again, wheezing into my microphone, 'Emma, we have him. Can you catch up? It might be someone you know.'

Her voice came back, 'Oh my, gosh, yes! I'm coming.'

I glanced over my shoulder to see that Emma was indeed now running in my direction and tried to up my pace.

The reason the bag snatcher didn't get to escape, and why Barbie didn't need to apprehend him, was because the stocky black woman was sitting on him. When he hit the pavement, she followed him down with an elbow to his gut, driving the air from his lungs and causing him to curl into a foetal position. He didn't get to stay there though because she then produced cuffs and had arrested him by the time Barbie coasted to a stop.

Two minutes later, when I got to them, huffing and puffing and probably looking like someone had shut me inside an industrial tumble dryer, the bag snatcher was sitting up with his legs crossed and his hands behind his back looking glum as Barbie, Jermaine, and the new woman talked.

The woman had a radio in her hand, talking to someone at the other end. 'Yeah, it's Benny again.'

'I wanna claim police brutality,' Benny whined from the floor.

The woman took the radio away from her mouth for a moment, then used her spare hand to flick the tip of his ear. 'Shut up, Benny.'

'What's going on?' I whispered to Barbie.

Barbie leaned her head my way. 'She's a cop, I guess. I haven't seen her ID, but she was reading him his rights when I got here.'

The woman ended her message and dropped the radio into her bag. 'Hello. Is this your handbag?' she asked, offering me Emma's heavy brown handbag full of money.

'It's mine,' said Emma, also out of breath as she arrived.

The woman made no attempt to hand it back, reaching into her own bag to pull out a flip-over black wallet. 'I'm PC Woods. This P.O.S at my feet is Benny Beans. He likes to steal things, don't you Benny?' She nudged him with her foot, making him harrumph and try to shuffle away from her. 'This is the third time I have arrested Benny this month. I ought to have a reward card or something; like you get caught nine times and you get to go free on the tenth.'

'Yeah, that's sounds good,' said Benny, instantly warming to the idea.

PC Woods rolled her eyes. 'There's a car on the way, Benny. I don't think they are going to let you out this time.'

'Can I have my bag back?' asked Emma.

'You'll have to come to the station for it. Sorry. It is evidence, so I have to catalogue it.' She looked apologetic, disappointed the victim had to get further messed about.

Approaching fast footsteps brought my attention around to a pair of uniformed cops approaching from the Fremlin Walk direction we had come from. I recognised one of them but had to dredge my memory to recall his name.

'PC Hardacre?' I asked as he and his colleague got close enough for normal speech volume.

He had been looking at Benny, but swung his eyes to me now, doing the same thing I had to recall a name. 'Mrs Fisher, right?'

'Yes.' Jermaine and Barbie were looking for me to explain. 'He took my statement at Charlie's house when Emily tried to kill us both.'

'Oh, hey!' gasped PC Woods. 'I thought I recognised you. You're the woman who fell off the stage during that big hoo-hah in Zangrabar,' she sniggered. 'That's exactly the same kind of stupid thing I would do.'

I didn't think she was laughing at my expense, despite how it looked. I thought perhaps she was trying to empathise with me.

PC Hardacre interrupted to save us all. 'Working plain clothes again, Patience?' he asked PC Woods.

'Yeah. It suits me,' she smiled. 'This fine ass wasn't made to wear that dowdy uniform you have on.' She certainly was a character.

There seemed to be very little else to say or do. Benny was an opportunistic thief, snatching a handbag because it looked tempting. Had he known there was ten thousand pounds in it, he might have run a little faster, but he wasn't connected to the dognapping and Emma still hadn't received a message from the mysterious person who brought her to Maidstone.

She was quite tearful.

Emma was going to walk to the station, less than half a mile away at the other end of the shopping area. I was going back to the drawing board. We came in one car, the Bentley this time because it would have been a squeeze in the Aston Martin or the Mini. Jermaine drove, which suited me, but I wanted to go to the office now. I had rented the place and furnished it but barely been there since. The client meets, one of the key purposes for the office, usually took place at the client's house.

However, I had one today at five o'clock and I was pleased to be going there for a few hours. Back at the house, I collected Anna. The puppies were already weaning and would not miss her. In a few weeks they would be going to new homes so the process of getting her used to being separate from them had to be started. I felt like I was tearing her away from them, but she couldn't have been happier to leave them behind.

With her on the passenger seat, we set off for the office in my silver Aston Martin.

Weird Things at the Office

The office sat in the old part of Rochester High Street and about thirty yards from the back of the cathedral, as the street ran behind it. Rochester High Street was a magical place where the Elizabethan architecture had been maintained. If one removed the neon signs outside the kebab shop and got rid of the traffic lights in the distance at the bridge end, one could easily imagine it was two hundred years ago.

At night, the alleyways running between the tightly packed buildings were dark and one could easily apply the word foreboding. It was always busy though, lots of restaurants and bars making it quite wonderful after dark. I had all but forgotten its delights until I rented the office.

There were two appointed parking spaces behind the office, both of which were empty, no one cheekily choosing to use them because I wasn't. This was the first time I had brought Anna here since the very first time I viewed it. She remembered though, pulling me to the door to then stare at it as if it might magically open.

Upstairs, while Anna sniffed everything, I settled at the computer and prodded it into life. Then I noticed the envelope on my desk. That was strange; the door was locked. How had it got there? Did Mr Jarvis still have a key? Almost certainly, I told myself, answering my own question, but then had to ask why he would let himself in and leave a letter on my desk.

I picked it up to look at it, employing my detective skills to note that it was good quality paper and had been hand delivered, not mailed as there was no stamp and the envelope was marked only with my name. Elegantly handwritten, using black ink from a fountain pen, the rear of the envelope was sealed with wax which had been embossed with a stamp. It was all very proper.

I set it to one side and clicked the mouse on the computer to bring it to life. Then I opened my emails to see what I might have. Jermaine hadn't had time to open each one and sift them for me yet today, so I had over a hundred to go through. That sounded remarkably boring, reinforcing the idea of having an assistant who dealt with such mundane tasks. I pursed my lips, told myself to get on with it and promptly put the task off to make a cup of tea.

As the kettle boiled – the first time it had ever been pressed into service - I looked around the small office and wondered what secrets it might be able to share. None probably, since the whole thing had apparently burned to the ground before being renovated, but if it could talk, it might have all manner of tales. The building was hundreds of years old, but what was its original purpose? Who were the first people to step into this room? I wandered to the window to look out at the people walking by in the High Street outside. Snorting a small laugh at myself, I realised I was staring at a pub along the street. They would have cold gin and that sounded a lot better than hot tea.

I took my place back at my desk a minute later, cracked my knuckles and willed myself to deal with the message inbox. The envelope begged my attention though. I hadn't opened it because the pretty red wax thing on the back was something I had only ever seen on television and I didn't want to break it. At home I had a letter opener which would slice along the top edge, preserving the integrity of the envelope while also exposing its contents. Maybe I could achieve the same with a nail file.

I gave it a go, carefully sliding the tool up against the top flap of the envelope. It didn't want to cut; the paper was of such quality it refused to give until I added enough effort to overcome the resistance, at which point I tore the stupid envelop in half, ruining the wax seal as it exploded into fragments. Sighing, I plucked out the piece of paper inside.

The message stopped me cold and a terrifying sense of dread made my head spin.

Mrs Fisher,

It is with regret that I am forced to contact you. Recently, you chose to meddle in my affairs for a third time and it will be the last. Each of us has to have rules and standards by which we live. For me the guiding principle is family and you have hurt mine.

I was advised to deal with you after the first incident, but foolishly I thought better of it. I wrote it off as amateurish luck and admit I was impressed with you despite the damage you caused to my empire. Ruefully, I realised I could have saved us all a lot of heartache if I had just sunk that silly ship you were on.

Your death warrant was signed after the second incident, but you moved so swiftly to the third event, I was unable to act before you struck at me again. No more will be tolerated. The millions in lost revenue can be recouped, despite what my business partners think. However, it is the blatant disrespect for my organisation and what it stands for that angers me.

I'm afraid we will not meet, Mrs Fisher. It might please me to be there as you are dispatched but I deplore violence and have other, less annoying, matters to attend to.

You have one week to get your affairs in order.

L.L.

The Godmother

I read it three times, my pulse hammering in my chest as I tried to make sense of it. I didn't know who L.L. was though I assumed it was a she because it was signed as *The Godmother*. I also didn't have any idea what she was on about or what I might have done to incur her wrath.

Forcing myself to be calm, I said, 'It might just be a hoax, Patricia.' I was trying to talk myself down off a ledge. I have been threatened before. Many times, in fact, and usually in person, but somehow, the creeping dread from the hand-written letter was the worst.

My hand shook as I picked up my mug of tea and I needed both hands to take a sip. I had to talk to someone. I would call Mike Atwell; that was a good starting place. However, no sooner had I picked up my phone than the door at the bottom of the stairs opened.

Anna barked in response, rushing to the upper door where she had to stop because it was shut.

Terror gripping me, I looked at the letter again. She gave me a week to get my affairs in order and it was dated a week ago. Footsteps were coming up the stairs; hard-soled shoes on wood. I tried to get to my feet, but my legs disobeyed my commands. Was someone watching me? Had they seen me open and read the letter so now were on their way to end my life? My knees were weak and my whole body was shaking. What could I use as a weapon? Why didn't I have a shotgun in the office for exactly this sort of ridiculous encounter? I was utterly trapped, and I didn't even know why.

Anna barked again, sniffing at the gap under the door and I finally came to my senses. In the corner of the office was a door that led to a toilet. I hadn't gone through it yet save for the first time when Tony Jarvis, the owner, was showing me around, but it linked to his travel agent shop. I could escape through there. I just needed to move fast.

119

I darted forward to grab Anna and saw that I was already too late. The person was no longer on the stairs but already on the landing outside the door.

'Hello?' said a voice outside, just before knocking politely three times. 'Am I in the right place? The door handle turned, and a round face popped through the gap. It bore a smile which quickly fell as he took in my expression. 'Here, are you alright?' He pushed the door all the way open. 'I know CPR,' he announced, almost bounding into the room now. 'Let's get you sat down, shall we?

'Who are you?' I demanded, my voice coming out as a half-screamed shriek.

He reacted as if I had given him an electric shock; one second trying to usher me backward to a chair by the window, the next jumping backward away from the crazy woman as if I were about to start screaming.

He was no threat. I could see that. It was just taking me a moment to calm myself down again.

'I'm Jerry. Jerry Brock. I have a five o'clock appointment.' He made a big show of checking his watch. 'Sorry, I'm a few minutes early. I thought maybe you were having a heart attack. You were white as a sheet.'

Still holding Anna, I backed away with her clutched to my chest and flopped into one of the chairs. There were two of them arranged either side of a small table by the window overlooking the High Street. I bought them so I would have somewhere to speak to clients, and now I was doing just that.

He followed me across the room, his hands out to either side as if he expected me to faint or collapse and wanted to be ready to catch me. As he moved in closer, I held up a hand to stop him.

'I'm fine. I'm not having a heart attack or anything. I just…' what could I tell him? I wasn't going to admit I thought it was a hired hitman coming up my stairs. 'I just had some bad news, that's all. I should have been expecting you but lost track of time.'

Frowning with doubt, Jerry backed away a pace. 'If you're sure.'

'Yes. Yes, sorry.' I placed Anna on the floor and stood up so I could shake his hand. 'I'm Patricia Fisher, thank you for choosing me to investigate.' It was a line I had practiced but never yet delivered. Finding myself on unsteady ground, I wanted something rehearsed to say. 'Won't you please sit?'

Content that I wasn't in need of medical attention though not looking convinced by my lie about receiving bad news, he took the other seat at the table. 'Nice spot you've got here.' He was looking out the window at the street below. The view from the window provided a shot down the street and all the amazing architecture. It was getting late and the sun had begun to dip which meant it was bouncing off the rooftops in a spectacular fashion. I was seeing it for the first time too.

Pushing it to one side, I asked, 'Let's get down to business, shall we?' He settled into his chair as I opened my notebook to the page I wrote on last night. 'It's your daughter, Helena, you want me to find, yes?' I still felt super shaky but focusing on my client would help to settle my nerves. Then, when he was gone, I was going to drink a bucket of gin.

'That's right, Mrs Fisher. Her husband, Gerard, too. They both went to work last Tuesday but haven't been seen since and neither said anything about going anywhere to anyone.'

'You've already been looking into this yourself, clearly.'

'When the police expressed that I shouldn't worry, I started to worry. They had been missing three days when I started to question why I hadn't heard from her. By Monday, I had confirmed no one knew where they were and called the police. Last night I emailed you.'

I checked my notes. 'Helena works at Swisscon in King's Hill. Has she been there long? Do you know if she is happy there?'

'Yes. If you are wondering if maybe she just decided to abscond from her job, then I want to express how unlikely I feel that is. She just got a promotion and she has been there for years.' I could hear the frustration in his voice; he had already explained everything many times to many people.

I knew where they worked; simple details like that were easy to come by, so I spent the next forty minutes asking about clubs and hobbies, friends, habits, and anything else I could think of. I got their mobile numbers and would get Barbie and Jermaine to help me widen the search net through their social media profiles later. It was a full background picture. All I had to do now was dig and keep digging until I found a clue to their whereabouts.

'Is there anything else you can think of?' I asked. It was my final question now that I had exhausted all the others.

Jerry thought for a second, scrunching his face up as he dredged his brain. 'I don't think so,' he concluded. 'If I do, I'll call.'

'Thank you. I will get started on this straight away, Jerry. I just need you to sign some paperwork.'

'Oh, yes. You told me that. You want a deposit too.'

We dealt with the formalities and there was nothing left to keep him in my office, however, he was hovering by the door. I could see he still had a question to ask. When I looked at him, he said, 'Do you think she's alive?'

This was tricky to answer. I didn't want to give him false hope, but if I suggested I thought it unlikely, then I was just taking his money for no reason. 'I think we should assume they are until we know otherwise. I will call you each day with an update.'

He thanked me for the dozenth time and left, clomping down the wooden stairs again to get back to the street. Alone once more, I picked up the letter and read it for the fourth time. I had no idea what it meant but I was certain it was nothing good. It could be a prank, but I didn't think it was. It couldn't be ignored, that was for sure, so later I would be doing what I could to find out who the Godmother was. The title was silly, like someone was ripping off the Godfather but failed to spot that they sounded like they ought to have a role in Cinderella.

Fairy Godmother. I would have smiled if it wasn't all so terrifying.

Anna made a noise by my feet. I looked down to find her looking up at me. She chomped her mouth at me, a sign that she expected me to do something that I ought to already be doing.

'It's dinner time, isn't it?' Anna spun on the spot and chomped her mouth at me again. I was getting hungry too. It was time to get home, but just as I grabbed my handbag and keys, my phone rang, displaying the name Mike Atwell.

'Hi, Mike. I'm glad you called actually. I need to show you a letter I just received.'

'Patricia, hi,' he said quickly, his tone putting me on alert. 'Are you busy? I'm at Emma Maynard's place, she says she's a client of yours. It's that dognapping case you were asking me about, isn't it?'

'Yes. Mike, what's wrong? What's happened?'

Sensing that he was scaring me, he quickly told me, 'She's fine. No harm to her. It's her house. It was broken into this afternoon. The place is trashed and vandalised.'

Emma's House

Forgetting the worrying letter from the Godmother, I raced to Emma's house, startled by the news of a break in and vandalism. She had been out for the last several hours, first at the ransom drop that never happened, and then at the police station making a statement about Benny Bean and getting her handbag back.

Then she finally arrived home to find her house had been invaded. I was feeling sorry for the poor girl when it suddenly occurred to me that the two events were linked. That made my right foot even heavier as I powered my way back to East Malling, thankful the traffic was being kind.

There were two squad cars outside the house when I pulled up. Anna got to her paws to look out the window, her tail wagging with excitement. 'You have to stay in the car, sweet girl.' She would not be welcome at a crime scene even if I held her, but she did her best to make me feel guilty by whining plaintively when I walked away.

Joshua Clifton, the boy who used to deliver my papers a decade ago, was standing at the open door, light from inside spilling out as the evening began to claim the daylight outside. Flashes popped as someone inside took pictures.

'Hello, Mrs Fisher,' said Joshua as I made my way up the path. 'DS Atwell said you would be along. Go right in. They are all in the back.'

I called out to get their attention as I went in, passing Joshua's partner, Marvin Gaye, who was in the kitchen making tea.

The back half of her house, plus a large conservatory that extends from it, is dedicated to her artwork, acting as studio and gallery. I knew that already from my previous visit. Coming past the kitchen, along a narrow hallway, an open doorway to my right showed me her living room. The first thing my eyes fell upon was the far wall where, in huge letters, was a single sprayed word: Slut.

It wasn't a nice word at any time, but to have it painted on your wallpaper was terrible. Would she ever be able to look at the wall again and not see it?

Mike heard me calling from the front door so found me staring into Emma's living room. Over my shoulder he said, 'The studio is worse.'

Wordlessly, I followed him through to the back of the house. He was right, it was much worse. 'Where's, Emma?' I asked since she wasn't in the room.

'Upstairs. She took herself to bed. I sent one of the uniform girls to keep an eye on her.'

I doubted the female police officers appreciated being referred to as girls, but I let it go without comment. That Emma had gone to lie down wasn't a surprise when I looked around what used to be a gallery displaying her work. Someone had torn it apart. Every single piece of artwork had been destroyed; frames were broken, her paints, brushes and other products were all wrecked. To add to that, every wall had something unspeakable written on it.

Two middle-aged gentlemen with plastic toolboxes came through the door behind me. They wore badges proclaiming them to be part of the Kent Police Forensic Science department.

Mike saw them. 'Hey, guys.' He waved and crossed the room to shake their hands.

'It's a bit of a mess,' said the first. Both looked very similar in that they had very little hair left on their heads, were the same height, both around fifty years old and it didn't help that they were wearing almost identical outfits of black trousers, white cotton shirt and a police issued windproof jacket with SOCO emblazoned on the back. The only way I was going to remember which was which was because one wore glasses.

Mike would remember to introduce me eventually, but I wasn't waiting for that. 'Hi,' I said as I stepped forward and into their line of sight. 'I'm Patricia Fisher.'

Both men looked at me. 'So you are,' said the one without the glasses who had already spoken. 'I'm Simon Barnshaw.' We shook hands.

His colleague with the glasses leaned forward to shake my hand as well, 'And I'm Steven Vines. Very pleased to meet you.'

Mike cut in. 'It's just what you see chaps. Prints and fibre if you can find any.'

'Burglary gone wrong?' asked Steven, looking around at the destruction and graffiti.

Mike shook his head which surprised me. 'The owner claims that nothing has been taken. This was all about doing damage. I've never seen anything like it.'

'Nor I,' remarked Simon, putting his toolbox down. 'We'll have to kick you out now.' He was shaking out an all in one set of overalls. They were thin white plastic – a forensic suit. 'This won't take long.'

Steven made a barrier by holding both arms out to his sides and ushered us back out into the hall.

'Nothing was taken?' I asked as Steven shut the door.

Mike huffed out a breath. 'Apparently. Miss Maynard was quite adamant about it. She even showed me her jewellery and a box she keeps cash in. Both were untouched so this was just about vandalism. What isn't clear is whether it was a random act by kids or perpetrated by someone who holds a grudge against her for something.'

'It was personal,' I replied as I slumped back against the wall a little. Mike tilted his head, ready to listen to me explain. 'This afternoon she was called to a meeting in Maidstone town centre where she was to hand over money and get her dog back. The dognapper never showed up and didn't bother to message again as he said he would. This happened while she was there – the message sending her to Maidstone was just to make sure she was out of the house so they could do this.'

Mike frowned but didn't argue. 'Any idea who is behind it?'

I blew out a frustrated breath. 'Not yet. The boyfriend is the most likely suspect still. He was the one I pegged as the prime suspect in the dognapping. I don't understand what the vandalism is about though. I think their relationship existed in the bedroom and nowhere else so unless she has been lying from the start, which I don't think she has, then I cannot perceive a reason for all this effort. It feels like revenge – like someone is punishing her.'

'We should talk to her.' Mike was already heading for the stairs.

I followed him up and around the landing to a door where a light shone out. The light inside was on but turned down dim. Emma was laying on her side on the bed looking dazed. In a chair at the foot of the bed was PC Patience Woods from earlier in town.

Mike knocked on the door frame as he went in. 'She's not saying much,' Patience advised Mike before turning her attention to me. 'You get about.'

I returned her smile. 'I could say the same of you. In uniform now?'

'Yeah. They make me do actual work when the shops shut. I like the shoplifter patrol; that's my favourite. Sometimes I don't catch anyone, and I get to spend all day shopping and drinking in coffee shops.'

Mike frowned his disapproval, but it seemed to bounce right off her. He had gone to the head end of the bed next to Emma and was kneeling, the motion clearly uncomfortable on his old knees. 'Emma, is there anything you can tell us that might help us catch whoever did this?'

She didn't move her head or attempt to make eye contact. She was staring into nothing when she said, 'No. No, I have no idea who would want to do this or why. They destroyed everything. Years of work. All my stock. Why would they do that?'

Mike didn't have an answer any more than I did. 'Mrs Fisher mentioned a boyfriend. Did your relationship end badly?'

She continued to stare at the wall. 'It wasn't like that. He just stopped calling and wouldn't answer my calls. We didn't fall out or anything like that. There was no argument. I don't think this is him.'

'Who could it be?' Mike asked.

I got in a question of my own before she could answer. 'Did the dognapper send another message yet?'

At the sound of my voice, Emma finally moved, taking her eyes off the wall to look down the length of the bed to where I was standing. 'Mrs Fisher I don't think I can employ you anymore. Nothing you have done so far has helped me in any way. I'm sure you were trying to help but I went to town on your advice today. Now things are worse than ever.'

129

I bit my lip, unsure how to answer but refusing to argue. I already felt responsible; not that I could have known the vandalism would happen, but it had, and I had failed to predict it.

When I didn't respond, she said, 'Please leave, Mrs Fisher.'

Feeling ashamed and small, I turned around and walked out of the room. I had been dismissed. It was a rude thing to do but I couldn't hold it against her. I was providing a service for which she was paying, and I could not claim she was getting her money's worth. I would solve this case, find out who destroyed her artwork and vandalised her house and I would get her dog back, doing all of it for free now that she had taken the case away from me.

There wasn't much more I could do here. Maybe Steven and Simon would find fingerprints that would lead to an arrest and the case would unravel before I got to solve it. That would be fine too. I didn't need it to be me; my pride wasn't such that I had to be the one to win every time.

I wanted to wait for Mike so I could show him the Godmother letter and ask him about it, but I had no way of knowing how long he might be upstairs talking to Emma. Pondering whether to wait or just head home where I would feel safe enough with Jermaine and could research the crazy Godmother myself, I spotted Janice Porter looking out of her window. She was backlit by the lights in her house as she made no attempt to hide that she was watching proceedings across the road.

She appeared startled when she saw me looking directly at her, as if I had caught her doing something wrong. I waved and started toward her. Anna saw me and barked; no doubt getting annoyed at the lack of dinner thus far this evening. I would remedy that as soon as we got home, but for now, I opened the car and took her with me.

Janice came to the door. 'Hi, Janice. I don't suppose you saw anything today, did you? Anyone near the house when they shouldn't be? Anyone new in the street?'

'You make it sound like I spend my days watching the neighbours,' she complained. She didn't put much conviction in it though because we both knew that was exactly what she did. I hoped to use her nosiness to my advantage. She sighed as she accepted her guilt and said, 'I didn't see anyone. My Kara went out with one of her emo friends just after two o'clock and I was in the garden trimming back the roses. Their season is well over now, so I wanted to prune them for next year. I should have done it weeks ago.' I thought I was going to get a horticultural lesson for a moment, but that was all she had to say on the matter.

'So, you didn't see anything and there's no point asking your daughter because she was out.'

'That's about it. Did they take much?' she asked, assuming it was a burglary.

'I couldn't possibly say. If you do think of anything, please call me. You have my card.' I bade her a good evening and left her to her evening, heading back to my car to get home. Anna needed feeding and I needed a gin and tonic. It was a disappointing day so far, but gin would smooth off some of the rough edges.

'Patricia.' Mike's call reached me just as I was about to get in my car. I figured he was still tied up with Emma, but he was hanging out of the door now. When I paused, half in, half out of my car, he let go of the doorframe to jog over to me.

It gave me the chance to show him the letter, which I fished out of my bag just as he arrived.

'Oh, what's that?' he asked as I made it clear I wanted him to see it.

'You first,' I replied, giving him the chance to say what it was he sought me out for.

'Oh, I just wanted to say that I would be interviewing the neighbours. I'm just about to send the uniforms door to door to see if anyone saw or heard anything. It can't have been easy to make this much mess without someone hearing something. They had to force the back door too. It looks like they used a crowbar to get it open. Anyway, if I turn anything up, I'll let you know.'

It was really good of him; he didn't have to offer his help. 'Thank you, Mike.'

'So, what's the letter?' he asked again.

I thrust it toward him. 'Here, read it.' He fished in a pocket for reading glasses, moving the pages around until they came into focus. I stayed quiet and watched as his eyes danced back and forth and down the page, his lips moving slightly as he read the words to himself.

He looked up when he got to the bottom. 'Do you know who it is from?'

I shook my head. 'Whoever L.L. is. I don't recall meeting anyone with those initials and I don't know who the godmother is. I don't even know what three events she is alluding to. I have meddled in her affairs and cost her millions.' I repeated her words.

He was rereading it as I spoke. 'She gives you a week to get your affairs in order and it is dated a week ago.' He looked up again to find me biting my lip nervously. An air of threat had put me on edge, and I felt like I was being watched. It was all I could do to avoid looking around continuously.

'Have you seen anyone watching you? Anyone following you? The same car in the same spot too many times?'

I had already quizzed myself on the same questions. 'Nothing like that at all. I wasn't looking for it though. I will be now. What are the chances this is a hoax or a prank?'

He shrugged. 'It could be. We should treat it seriously until we know which it is though. I want to show this to Chief Inspector Quinn. He is the local expert on organised crime. He will know who to speak to about the godmother. The godmother?' he repeated himself, screwing up his face at the name. 'It makes her sound like she escaped from a Disney film.'

'I know, right?' We both laughed, the mental image of a gangland megaboss with fairy wings and a wand sneaking into my head. 'I bet she has a special punishment for anyone who ever dares to mention it.'

'Yeah,' cackled Mike, 'She turns them into a pumpkin!' Now we were both howling, Joshua, still standing at Emma's door, giving us an odd look.

Calming down, Mike said, 'Can you hold it. I'll take a picture for now. Then can you bring it in to the station tomorrow so we can get a copy?'

'Sure.' I held up the single page so he could snap a picture. Anna barked her impatience at me, pawing at my leg as I hung out of the car still. 'Sorry, Mike. I really must get this one home for her dinner. It's two hours overdue now.'

He slid his phone away and took off his reading glasses. 'Sure thing. Have a good evening. Don't worry too much about the letter, it might be nothing.'

I waved him goodnight as I got into the car and plopped Anna on the passenger seat. He told me not to worry but I couldn't help myself from feeling concern. It was an enigma that I couldn't understand.

Had I known the truth I would have found somewhere to hide.

The house was ablaze with lights when I pulled off the road and onto the winding driveway. I could see it through the trees as I approached, and then, when I came out from under the canopy it was there before me, imposing and impressive.

It was the first time I had ever seen it at night. Now that the evenings were drawing in, I could appreciate what it looked like with the lights on. There were lights outside to cover the area in front of the doors and spotlights buried in the ground to illuminate the house. They were only shining onto the front façade but that was enough. I could only imagine what visitors thought when they arrived.

I pulled the car to a stop right in front of the step that led to the front door, which opened as I was getting out of the car. 'Come on, little girl,' I cooed at Anna. 'Let's get you some dinner and see if those puppies of yours have missed you.' She looked excited about the first thing but not so much about the second. She bounded away up the steps leaving me behind, running straight past Jermaine to find her food bowl. She would be mightily disappointed when she discovered it was still empty and waiting for me to fill it.

'Good evening, madam,' Jermaine greeted me as I climbed the steps. 'Has your evening been more successful?'

I gave him a rueful smile. 'Not really. I have a new case though, that's something.'

I was through the front door now and shucking my coat. Jermaine took it, flicked it once to shake out any creases and deftly swung it onto the coat hanger he held pinned beneath his right arm. As it went into a large, walk-in closet near the front door, he asked, 'Will Madam require an evening meal? Mrs Ellis prepared several options before she departed this evening.'

'Madam requires an industrial strength gin and tonic. After that, yes, some dinner would be wise.'

Barbie appeared on the grand sweeping stairs as I made my way to the pantry to make sure Anna got fed and her puppies were all okay. 'Patty, I messed up.' She looked worried.

Jermaine and I both stopped so she could get down the stairs to us. 'What is it?' I asked.

Her cheeks were burning with embarrassment. 'I ordered the cable to get that phone we found working. You know, the one in Edward Foy's climbing bag?' I kept quiet so she could deliver the news. 'I was supposed to get next day delivery, but I didn't tick the box like I thought I had so it's not coming until tomorrow morning.'

I waited, expecting more. When no more came, I asked, 'That's it? That's what has you worried?'

'Yeah,' she admitted coyly. 'I thought the phone was important.'

I smiled at her. 'Come on, gym bunny. I need a drink.' As we walked, I said, 'The phone might be important. It might not be. When will the cable come?'

She produced her phone. 'The tracking thingy says tomorrow between eight and nine.'

'That will have to do then. Chances are there will be nothing on it anyway. He didn't have a charger with it; maybe it had been in there since that kind of phone was new and he had forgotten it. We'll power it up to find a five-year-old text message about not forgetting to buy broccoli.' I

136

laughed at my own joke and was glad to have something to smile about if only for a few seconds. Things were not going well.

'Anything from the Wessex's?' I asked Jermaine as we got to the kitchen. Anna was already in there dancing around by the cupboard her food is kept in. Her puppies had all tumbled out of the open pantry door and were jumping around her, bouncing off one another as they played. So she could eat in peace, I picked Anna up, placing her on the counter while she chowed through her kibble.

In the meantime, Jermaine rescued bottles of gin and tonic from the refrigerator and made drinks for all three of us. Jermaine explained what Simon Wessex had told him earlier over the phone. The quickdraw had almost certainly been tampered with but there was more to it than that.

'What does that mean?' asked Barbie.

I sipped my gin and waited for his answer. 'They didn't say. He did confirm that an expert from the manufacturer in Boulder, Colorado was flying in to examine it. I have arranged to meet them at their shop in the morning unless you have other tasks for me, madam.'

Anna finished her kibble, licked her nose and belched. Barbie giggled and picked her up for a cuddle.

'No, Jermaine. I think you should go. I will be focusing on this case now. I just got fired from the other one,' I explained, remembering that they didn't know yet. 'Emma Maynard's house was broken into and trashed while we were in Maidstone. The whole ransom exchange thing appears to have been a ruse to get her out of the house.'

Barbie's hand shot to her mouth. 'Those sneaky little...'

'Yes, quite. I still don't have the faintest idea who took her dog or why... I don't blame Emma for cancelling my contract. Then there's this,' I said, taking the letter from my bag and placing it on the counter so they could read it. 'Whoever wrote this clearly believes I know who they are.

I stepped back a pace so Barbie and Jermaine could squeeze in and read it together. Just like with Mike Atwell, I watched their eyes dance left and right and down line by line to get to the bottom of the page, their eyes and eyebrows showing when they got to certain parts.

'The godmother?' questioned Barbie. 'Like... she's a fairy?' I wanted to laugh but it just wasn't funny.

Jermaine straightened up to his full height, a dangerous set to his eyes. He saw me as his principal; someone he was to protect at all times. 'Madam, do you know which three incidents this L.L. alludes to?'

I leaned on the counter and shook my head sadly. 'I wish I did. I don't know what I did to upset this person and whether they genuinely intend me harm or not. Mike Atwell is going to use contacts within the police to see if they can identify who she is. If we can work that part out, I might be able to do something about it.'

Barbie looked up from reading it again. 'She writes about sinking *the* ship. She must mean the Aurelia. Do you think this is to do with some of the things that happened when we were on board?'

'Very probably,' I replied. 'But what exactly, I couldn't say. She tells me it is three things. She let me off with the first, condemned me to death after the second and I got the third one in before she could have me killed. On the Aurelia was there anyone left who either didn't get killed or go to jail?'

We started to compile a list. It started with Mr Schooner, the former deputy captain.

'He went to jail in St Kitts. Last I heard, he was still there but awaiting trial. There was some debate over where he would be trialled and then imprisoned. That was being contested by the U.S. because the jewel theft was originally committed in America, but he didn't steal it though he did kill Jack Langley, an American citizen. He also killed Welshman Ian Davis in your suite so maybe the British want him for a murder trial. I could ask Deepa,' she said pulling out her phone. 'She'll be able to get us an answer.'

I nodded, staring into the distance as I remember the awful man and how close he came to having me locked up. It could be me still sweating in a jail in St Kitts accused of double murder. 'Yes, please do that.'

Jermaine spoke next, 'Then there was the incident with the Miami organised crime families. Very few of them were left alive though.'

'Eduardo Perez,' I murmured, saying his name for the first time in four months. 'He survived.'

'But he was taken away by the police,' Barbie pointed out.

'There were others,' I countered.

'But none with the initial's L.L.' argued Jermaine. 'That's hardly conclusive, of course, but none of the gangsters were women either.'

'Then there was Shane,' said Barbie, referring to the failed child actor who went on to claim several lives before he was stopped. 'He died though, so I guess he's probably not behind this.'

'I sure hope not,' I agreed. 'The Yakasi and Zanooza were almost all arrested. They might have the clout to come after me again though if they wanted to.'

'Surely not, madam,' argued Jermaine. 'The brothers blamed each other for their downfall.'

Jermaine was right. We ran through another half dozen possible enemies I might have attracted. People that found themselves in jail because I revealed their crimes. None of them seemed very likely. After half an hour of back and forth, two more gins and a chicken salad the three of us prepared together, we had no suspects. Whoever L.L. was, she remained an enigma for now.

Wondering what new enemy I now had coming for me kept me awake half the night.

Barbie and I stayed in the house to exercise the following morning. I like to jog but it was raining hard enough to dissuade me from venturing out. The house had a gym though which is not surprising when one considers the number of rooms it contained. At some point in the building's past, someone thought it would be a good idea to convert a room and then fill it with torture devices.

'We'll start on the climbers, shall we?' asked Barbie, walking up to a machine that stood almost vertical. It had feet stirrups and handles so the poor victim got on and started climbing, hand, foot, hand, foot, constantly moving the stirrups and handles up as they tried to fall down. By coordinating one's effort, a person could stay in the same spot perpetually, never getting to the top, never getting anywhere, except I would always arrive at a place called exhausted and sweaty.

'How's about no?' I tried. 'I hate the climber.'

Barbie just giggled at me. 'That's why we should do it, Patty. The best exercises are always the ones we don't want to do.' She was already climbing onto the left-hand machine so, reluctantly, I boarded its twin and began climbing.

She leaned across to adjust the resistance which meant I had to go faster to stay off the ground. 'Don't want it to be easy,' she quipped. 'What would be the point of that?'

A minute later, her arm reached across to turn the resistance up even higher but this time I growled at her and tried to bite her hand. She pulled it back quickly, laughing at me again.

Twenty minutes later we switched to a rowing machine and then a spin bike. I used the walls a lot to get back to my room to shower and change; my legs refusing to cooperate. I always felt great an hour after my workouts, just never during or before or immediately afterward.

Applying a swipe of eye make-up as my last touch, the mirror was generous enough to make me look less tired than I felt, but as I made my way down to breakfast, I had to wonder what I was going to do today. I had a new case from Jerry Brock to get started on and I still wanted to solve the dognapping case even though the client had removed me from it. I also still needed to apply effort to Edward Foy's case. I was four days in now and still hadn't worked out if he was murdered or not though the (probably) sabotaged quickdraw would suggest he had. The crime, if I assumed it was not an accident, appeared to have no motive. He was a loving husband and a good stepfather to Susie. Angry teenager or not, she hadn't a bad word to say about him.

Usually, I found that I had a sense for what could have happened, as if the pieces of the puzzle, jumbled as they always are, would align for me to show me the answers. With Edward's case, just like Emma's missing dog, I was lost, and it worried me.

Melissa was bringing Sam over at nine this morning, which stopped me from going out. But I had an hour or so before they were due, so I could start using the information I got from Jerry Brock to find my way into his missing persons case and hope I had better luck with that.

'Good morning, madam.' Jermaine's deep rumbling bass broke me from my thoughts as I descended the stairs. He wore his full butler's livery complete with tails and white gloves. There was absolutely no need for it, so he wore it for his own pleasure. Guiltily, I admit that I wanted other people to visit the house and see him wearing it; Angelica Howard-Box perhaps. She would then feel a need to hire someone who she would then treat like a slave though, and I couldn't imagine a scenario where I would allow her to enter my house, so it was never likely to happen.

'Good morning, Jermaine dear. I thought you were travelling to Sandwich this morning.'

'Yes, madam. I will change out of my livery before I travel.'

'Which car will you take?' I asked him with a conspiratorial smile.'

He couldn't stop his own face from smiling when he said, 'The Bentley. It is rather nice to drive.'

'I shall have to have a go myself.'

'It is your car, madam,'

As we reached the kitchen together, I said, 'I prefer to think of the cars as belonging to the house. I didn't buy any of them and I certainly don't feel any sense of ownership. Except maybe the Aston Martin.' That one I had picked.

Anna appeared from the pantry, tailed by four tiny puppies, as she came to see me, and they followed. I crouched to make a fuss of them all, but Anna really only wanted her breakfast.

'She's been fussing for food ever since I arrived, Mrs Fisher,' said Mrs Ellis, taking a loaf from the oven. The kitchen smelled divine; fresh coffee and freshly baked bread filling the air and making my stomach rumble its emptiness.

Barbie was at the small table with a bowl of quinoa and berries, a spoon dangling from her mouth. We could eat in the dining room, but this wasn't Downton Abbey despite being about the same size, and I preferred the homey feel I got from the warmth and smells of the kitchen.

In Barbie's hands was Edward Foy's phone. 'I can't get it to work,' she told us, dropping the spoon back into her bowl. 'It is beginning to annoy me.'

I looked in her bowl. 'Is there more of that?' Barbie tended to bulk make her meals. She didn't let Mrs Ellis make anything for her after catching her adding a pound of butter to a skillet which she then intended to fry some shrimp in.

Barbie didn't look up from poking the phone but pointed to the refrigerator. 'There's a big bowl on the second shelf. Just add whatever yoghurt and berries you fancy.'

I fed Anna, and the puppies; they were on a special puppy food now, two to a bowl and more excited even than mum to get their share of it. As they fell silent to focus on getting as much of the meaty mix as possible, I took my own bowl of quinoa and berries and sat next to Barbie so I could see what she was doing.

'It might be dead,' she announced.

'Chances are there was nothing on it anyway. It was a long shot.'

'Yeah. But you said you don't have anything else to go on, Patty.'

Jermaine looked over her shoulder. 'It might just need longer for the charge to activate it.'

Huffing in her frustration, Barbie scraped up the last of her breakfast, pushed back her chair and took the phone and cable with her. 'I'll plug it in at work and see if it does anything if I just leave it alone for a while.'

'Good plan,' said Jermaine.

Barbie grabbed a backpack from the floor, stuffed the phone and charger into it and then air-kissed us both before dashing from the room.

'Where does that one get her energy?' asked Mrs Ellis.

Deadpan, I replied, 'She's twenty-two.' Mrs Ellis nodded in acknowledgement. Like me, Barbie's age was so far behind us that she couldn't remember what she felt like at that age.

The doorbell rang, the sound echoing through the relative quiet of the house. In the distance, Barbie's voice followed it. 'There's someone at the door. Shall I let them in?'

I smirked when I saw Jermaine move faster than his usual glacial butler's pace. He might have catlike reflexes and be able to move faster than light when he wanted to, but back on the Aurelia, whenever anyone came to the door of my suite, he crossed the room to answer it at a dignified snail's pace, never being hurried by someone else's urgency. Now, with the threat that Barbie might answer the door when it should be him, he was forced to hurry.

I followed behind to see what he did as he neared the door and caught him slowing to his usual snail's pace for the last few steps. I expected guests so it was no surprise when he opened the door to show Melissa and Sam inside.

Mrs Ellis had snuck along behind me, curiosity making her leave the kitchen to see why I was being surreptitious. 'Wherever did you find him, Mrs Fisher? In all the years I have worked here, I have never seen a butler so dedicated to his duties.' Then she saw who was coming in. 'Oh, is that Sam Chalk and his mum?'

'Yes.' I stepped out from the corner we were peering around. 'I invited him over to see the puppies.'

145

Melissa saw me and waved. Sam waved too as I strode across the house's central hall. Staircases swept down on either side to meet the marble floor at the bottom about halfway along the expanse. Melissa was looking around with the same stunned face I had when I first stepped foot inside. Sam didn't seem to notice. For him, it was just a house.

'Hello, Mrs Fisher,' he called as he continued to wave.

'Madam, this is Mrs Melissa Chalk and her son Samuel Chalk.' Jermaine liked to announce people.

'Thank you, Jermaine.' I turned to Melissa, whose eyes were roving everywhere, trying to take it all in. 'There's fresh tea or coffee in the kitchen. Won't you please come in?'

They already were inside, but it seemed the thing to say, Jermaine's stuffy formality making me act and speak differently.

'This place is incredible,' gasped Melissa, her voice a reverent hushed whisper. 'I knew it was big; I drive by it all the time, but… wow.'

'What is it, mum?' asked Sam, confused about what she found so distracting and tugging at her hand in his eagerness to see the puppies.

I reached out my hand to take his. 'Have a look around if you like, Mel. I'll be in the pantry with Sam.'

I led him away, but she followed, gawping at the staircases and the marble floors and the giant mirrors and everything else her gaze fell upon.

Anna appeared before we reached the pantry, hearing new voices and assuming that meant someone to fuss her. Three puppies tumbled after, big enough now to clamber over the four-inch-high barrier Mrs Ellis put at the bottom of the pantry door to keep them in. Only Georgie was left, yipping in her frustration at being left behind.

146

'Oh, wow,' said Sam, getting onto the floor so the puppies could climb on him. Ringo widdled in his excitement, causing me to reach for the kitchen towel before Sam sat in it. Mrs Ellis fished out Georgie and plopped her down with her brothers who were all clambering onto Sam now that they had a victim to climb and lick. It was a bit like seeing Gulliver pinned to the floor by the Lilliputians.

'Happy down there, Sam?' asked Melissa.

Sam just giggled.

Mrs Ellis held up the kettle. 'Tea, please,' said Melissa in response.

I added, 'Make that two, please.' Then I scooped up Anna. 'Mummy is a bit over having puppies now. I think she will be glad to let them go.'

'Do you have homes for them yet?' Melissa asked.

I shook my head. 'No. I haven't even really decided what I want to do. I can't keep them. Although I am rather taken by little Georgie. She's the only girl in the litter and the smallest, constantly pushed out by her brothers. If I let them go, I need to know they are going to good homes.'

'How much will you sell them for? I think Sam would enjoy having a dog.'

It hadn't occurred to me to suggest it. 'If you want one, then it is free. I indicated about the house. 'It's not like I need the money.'

'No, that's too much,' Melissa protested.

I held up a hand to stop her. 'You would be doing me a favour. I never intended for her to get pregnant. The little minx snuck out of my room in Zangrabar and found her way into the Queen's Corgis.'

'Wait. You're telling me these are royal puppies?'

I puffed out my cheeks as I considered how to answer. 'Not exactly. I mean, it was the Queen's dogs, but I don't think her dogs actually have titles conferred upon them.'

Melissa laughed. 'It's close enough for me. Thank you, I'll take one. Did you hear that, Sam? Patricia is letting us have one of the puppies. Do you want to help me pick?'

Sam had Paul standing on his face to lick his right eyeball. 'No thanks, mum. I already have a puppy.'

She squinted in confusion. 'There he goes again with talk about a puppy. What puppy, Sam? We don't have a puppy.'

'The one in the shed. I see it every day. It's my friend.'

It was at least the third time I had heard him claim to see a puppy and not the first time he told me it was in a shed. 'Sam, what sort of puppy is it?'

He rolled slightly and Paul fell off to land upside down on the floor. Sam chuckled at the clumsy dog just as it righted itself and tried to attack him again.

'Sam,' warned Melissa, employing a mum's tone. 'Mrs Fisher asked you a question. We always remember our manners, don't we?'

'Yes, mum,' said Sam as he sat up. 'Sorry, Mrs Fisher. It is a very small puppy.'

An old familiar itchy feeling crept over the back of my skull. It propelled me across the room to fetch my phone where a quick internet search produced a picture I could use. Crouching down to Sam's height on the floor, I showed him the screen. 'Does it look like this?'

He grinned a big goofy grin. 'Yes, that's my puppy.'

He knew where Horace was. He told me about it three days ago and I didn't listen. I could have solved the whole damned case at the start of the week. As realisation hit me, I straightened up again. 'Melissa, I need to borrow your son. Sam, can you show me where your puppy is, please? Show me which shed it is in?'

Melissa looked confused. 'What's happening?'

'I think Sam just solved a case for me. I need him to show me where the puppy is. Is that okay?'

A little taken aback, she said, 'Um, yes, of course. If that's alright with Sam.'

Sam clambered to his feet as well, carefully taking Dachshund puppies off to place them on the floor as he went. 'It's in the village. It's not far.'

Thinking fast about what I might need I turned to Mrs Ellis. 'Pam, can you find Tom, please. I think I will need him to come with me and ask him to bring some tools. I'll meet him in the garage.'

Then I was moving, my feet hurried as I felt the excitement rising. I had no way to be certain that Sam was giving me accurate information, but I didn't think it was in his nature to lie and… and what? I had some kind of special Patricia intuition that told me when I had solved a case even before I had? Something like that because I felt utterly certain I was about to find Horace.

Jermaine had left for Sandwich, so I had the terrible chore of finding my own coat and shoes. I tell you; life can be hard without a butler to hand. I didn't joke about it verbally though just in case Melissa thought I was being serious. I grabbed their coats as well and led them through the

149

house to the garage. In hindsight, I probably should have warned her because she uttered several extraordinary expletives when she saw the collection of cars.

'How many are there?' she asked with wide eyes.

Tom came in through a side door to save me from having to answer. 'Mrs Ellis said you might need some tools but didn't say what for, Mrs Fisher.' He had an armful of different things and a toolbox on wheels in one hand. One item I recognised was the most likely thing we would need.

'Are those bolt cutters?'

'They certainly are, Mrs Fisher.' They were five feet long and looked like they would eat through armour plate.

'We may need to break into a shed. It is probably locked with a padlock or something.'

'These will do it then. Which car are we taking?'

There were four of us plus the tools. 'The Range Rover?'

Horace

The Range Rover was an Overfinch model. I didn't know what that meant, I just saw the badge and figured it was a special edition of some kind. I was both right and wrong. Tom explained when he saw the shocked look on my face as I started the engine.

Overfinch was, in his words, the ultimate expression of luxury and power in a four by four vehicle. The firm took a stock car and dismantled it, replacing half the parts with uprated versions. The engine was now a supercharged five litre V8 powerhouse and all the suspension and brakes and other components were matched to take the power it could now deliver. I didn't know what most of that meant but I knew this; it sounded like an angry dragon and took off like a gazelle with a firework tied to its tail.

Whoever supplied the cars to the Maharaja's collection knew their stuff, that was for sure.

Sam told us the shed was at the edge of the allotments. Between the old part of the village, where Melissa lived, and the new part, where one could find Janice Porter and Emma Maynard, was a chunk of woodland. However, on the side nearest the old part of the village was a long strip of allotments where families had been growing vegetables and keeping chickens for decades.

The woodland wasn't very big; maybe one hundred yards at the widest point and people, kids especially, often took a shortcut through it to get from one part of the village to the other. I parked behind Melissa's house as it backed right up to the allotments and we all followed Sam as he led us to the shed. I couldn't help keeping my fingers crossed as we wound around the muddy paths.

'Just you be careful of your new shoes, Sam,' called Melissa from the back of our little procession as she tried to pick her way around the puddles. I wished I had put wellington boots on, but it was too late for that now.

As Sam led us to the back of the allotments and turned right, I could see where we were going; there was only one shed in this direction. A small, run down, wooden thing with a sagging roof. The allotment itself hadn't been tended to this year and was overgrown with weeds and brambles. It looked abandoned.

'Puppy!' called Sam as we got near. 'Puppy!' There was no response at first, but as we got close, I heard what might have been a yip. 'There's a window around the side,' Sam pointed.

Sure enough, there was a window in the side and sitting inside on top of a pile of stored furniture, abandoned tools, and general detritus, was a tiny, little, teacup Yorkshire Terrier.

Sam had led me to Horace. 'Tom, would you be a dear and open the door for me?'

'Right you are, Mrs Fisher.' The door was secured with a hasp and staple held closed with a padlock. The padlock lasted about half a second against the bolt cutters, the door swinging open as Tom stepped back out of the way.

'Do you want to get him?' I asked Sam. 'You were the one who found him.'

His goofy grin still in place, Sam went into the shed and picked the tiny dog up. It looked nervous and I couldn't see a water bowl or food anywhere, but it clung to Sam as if he was its long-lost owner. A tag glinted through the fur around its neck, the name Horace etched into the surface when I checked it.

'I think we should take this one directly home.' I turned to Melissa. 'It that okay? I could do with Sam's help for a little while longer.'

'Do you need me?' she asked in reply.

'I don't think so. If you trust me with Sam, I'll bring him back when we are done.'

'Jolly good. I think I'll leave you to it and get on with some housework.' As Sam cuddled Horace to his chest, Melissa ruffled his hair. 'Well done, Sam. Be a good boy for Mrs Fisher.'

'Yes, mum.'

As she left, I turned to Tom. 'Tom, do you want to take the car back to the house? There's no sense in you traipsing after me.'

He raised his eyebrows. 'I wouldn't hear of it, Mrs Fisher. I shall walk back. It'll only take ten minutes. Although, if its alright with you, I'll leave the tools in the car and take them out when you bring it back.'

'Of course, Tom.' With that decided, I started into the woodland that divides the old part of the village from the new. Sam tagged along behind, holding Horace and jabbering away to him.

A few minutes later, and with considerably more mud on my shoes, we emerged from the trees with the newer houses ahead of us. I took out my phone to call Emma.

I wondered if she would even answer, but she did, sounding despondent and unhappy to be getting a call from me. 'If you are calling to see if I have changed my mind, then I haven't, Mrs Fisher.

153

'I have Horace,' I spoke over her before she could say anything else.

I got silence in response for several seconds before she repeated my words, 'You have Horace?'

'Yes, he was locked in a shed. If you look out your window you will see me coming along the street. I have a friend with me.'

Three seconds later, her front door burst open and Emma ran out into the street. She was barefoot but didn't seem to notice or care as she dropped her phone and ran to see if the bundle of fur Sam carried really was her dog.

She knew before she got to him because Horace saw her coming, barked and wriggled enough for Sam to have to put him down. The tiny dog sprinted to his owner, jumping into the air for her to catch him as she crouched. Sam and I got to watch the tearful reunion, keeping quiet as Emma cried and Horace licked her face.

When it began to subside and she stood up, I said, 'I think he might need food and water.'

'Oh, my God. Where was he? How did you find him? Who had him?' Her questions came in a torrent, but I didn't answer any of them, not straight away. Sam and I were following her to her house, but my feet had stopped moving. Across the street, in front of Janice Porter's house was a car I recognised. Or, rather, it was the sticker on the back which had lodged in my memory. The pink princess sticker was undoubtedly mass produced and sold for pennies but stuck to the back bumper of a ten-year-old Renault Clio, it had to be Susie Foy's car.

Gawping open-mouthed at it, I was oblivious to Emma speaking to me, and staring right at Janice Porter's house when the door opened. Kara came out followed by Susie Foy. They were both Emos, but that hadn't seemed like a reason to connect them; there were plenty of teenagers who dressed like them. They knew each other well enough to be riding around in the same car though.

Susie saw me staring at her and showed her class by giving me her middle finger and a sneer as she got into her car. As it powered away down the street leaving a trail of blue smoke, the familiar itch at the back of my skull returned.

I had missed something important.

'Mrs Fisher?' Emma's voice broke through my thoughts.

'Mmm? Sorry. I was thinking.'

Emma wore a frown. 'Do you know those girls?'

'Sort of,' I replied, still running through things in my head. Seeing them together meant something. I just didn't know what.

'I'm going inside to get Horace some water and to see if he wants to eat. Then I'm going to take him to the vets for a check-up. I was asking how you found him.'

'How I found him,' I repeated, barely hearing my own voice as I followed her into her house, my brain whirring madly. Inside, I did my best to explain that Sam had found him in a shed on the allotments. Horace hungrily vacuumed up a bowl of doggy meat while balanced on Emma's lap, his owner unwilling to put him down in case he proved to be a mirage. I found it difficult to concentrate on what I needed to tell her as I was too busy trying to piece together Susie and Kara and what that might mean. Several times I had to ask her to repeat a question.

Mercifully, she was in a hurry to get to the vets, where she planned to remain until they could see her. Without an appointment it might take a while, but I expected they would consider hers to be a special case.

I had to admit that I still didn't know who had taken Horace, or who the mysterious dognapper messages were from, nor who it was who trashed her house and destroyed her artwork. All in all, she hadn't got much for her money when she hired me. I didn't even find her dog; that was Sam. I would shortly find out who the allotment was leased by, that would give me someone to question at least. It looked like an abandoned plot though so it could be that the tenant knew nothing about the dog in their shed.

As she drove off to the vets in Kings Hill, Sam and I began the walk back to his house. We went the longer way around on the path rather than back through the woods where we would get even muddier.

Halfway there, my phone rang with some unexpected news.

'Patty, it's Barbie. I got the phone working. There's a whole bunch of messages on here. It looked like Edward Foy was playing around on his wife.'

'Are you at the gym?'

'Yeah.'

'Stay there, I'm coming to you.'

'I have a class in ten minutes.'

I hurried my pace. It wasn't possible to get there in ten minutes, but I was sure she would leave the phone at reception for me or something like that. Barbie worked in a big, plush health centre on the Kings Hill business estate. Lots of big firms had their headquarters there plus there were thousands of houses in the surrounding area so the gym was very busy all the time. They signed Barbie up for a job there about nine seconds after she walked in; at least that was the way she told the story. No interview required. She looked the part and had all the qualifications.

Nearing the Range Rover, I plipped it open with the key fob, planning to put my handbag in and then take Sam around the front to drop him off with his mum again. He got in though. As I dropped my handbag in the back and closed the door again, he was in the front and had his seatbelt on.

I opened the driver's door. 'I need to get you back to your mum.'

He grinned at me. 'I thought we were going to solve the case? That's what you kept saying on the way back.' He was right, I had been mumbling to myself, running different ideas through my head now that I had new information about Edward. He carried a phone in his climbing

157

bag and had been sleeping with other women. That changed several elements of the case. For a start, he wasn't the husband Sarah made him out to be, but if he was lying about one thing, was he also lying about his climbing habits? Did he free climb? Was he the safety conscious man she thought he was?

I gasped as an idea hit me. She knew about the infidelities and she tampered with his gear! I played the concept around in my head. There was a hole in the idea I could drive a bus through. She was the one saying it was murder. She was the one who hired me after the death by misadventure verdict was given.

'Mrs Fisher?' Sam's voice tugged me back to reality. I said a bad word and got in the car. I could return Sam later; I was too keen to see what was on the phone to mess around taking him into Melissa's now.

The mighty Overfinch engine roared to life and my right foot was a little heavy again as I powered out of the village. That was why I almost hit Angelica Howard-Box when I swung the big car around a turning just as she was getting to the junction. I made sure I didn't cut the corner, but I think she hadn't expected me, or anyone, and I was moving a little faster than I ought to be.

In a frozen split-second, she locked eyes with mine, then I was gone, rocketing down the road to the sound of her horn as it faded into the distance behind me.

I slipped the car into an empty parking space at the gym and dashed inside, Sam hot on my heels. Inside, we met a lady on the reception desk. The name on her badge was Shirley and Shirley liked donuts. Of a pack of six on her desk, there were only two left and she had sugar sticking to the fine hairs above her top lip.

'Good morning, welcome to Kings Hill Health and Fitness. Are you members?'

'Good morning. I'm a friend of Barbara Berkeley. Has she left anything for me?

'No. But she did tell me you would be coming, and I should have you escorted to her class. If you sign the visitor's book, I will buzz you through.' As I uncapped the pen and made my entry, she stood up from her chair to spot a member of staff and wave them over.

A teenage boy, who looked to be about seventeen and had an unfortunate rash of spots beneath his shock of ginger hair, jogged across to the desk. 'This is Patricia Fisher,' she told the boy, whose name badge said Todd. 'She's famous. Take her to Barbie's class and remember to talk to her face this time, okay?'

The boy went bright red, but wordlessly turned around and started to lead the way. I mouthed thank you to Shirley, yet another person who imagined me to be far more than I am, and followed Todd through a door that led to a corridor.

Thumping music escaped through a door on our left, which trebled in volume as Todd pushed it open. Inside, three dozen men and women of various ages looked about ready to die as sweat poured from them. Each was standing behind a mat and had a barbell above their heads. The barbells weren't very heavy, but I knew from painful experience how many times Barbie would expect them to be lifted into the air.

'Keep going!' screamed Barbie the evil dungeon master as heads turned our way. Todd went two paces inside the room and waited, his head and eyes looking way up to the ceiling so there was no chance he could be accused of looking at anything that wasn't her face.

Barbie put down her barbell, grabbed the phone from a pile of things behind her, and jogged across to us. 'Thank you, Todd, you can go.' Todd legged it for the door. 'I wasn't sure if you were familiar enough with this old model to get it to work, Patty, I figured I might as well show you.' Before I could answer, her head whipped around to scowl at someone who was trying to put his barbell down. 'Is that how you get fit, Zac?' she screamed. 'Is that how you erode your love handles? If you want to take it easy, stop eating pies!' then she turned back to me, the scowl replaced instantly by a pleasant smile. 'Here.' She pressed a couple of buttons to open the message app. 'Jermaine was right; it just needed to get more juice in it before it would start. I left it charging while I took a class and when I came back to check on it, it was working.' She handed it to me. 'These are his contacts.'

They were all women's names.

'If you open any of them, you will see the messages going back and forth.'

I pressed the first name, which as they were alphabetical, was Amanda. I only needed to read a few to determine that he was having sex with her. Next was Anastasia and the result of her messages with him was the same. Then Belinda. I was just about to stop looking when I noticed the E's. There was only one entry and it was an Emma.

The itchy feeling made me open the contact to see the messages and as Barbie shouted at Zac again, I almost dropped the phone. The most recent message was from just a couple of days ago.

Damian, I realise you have decided you can't be bothered with me anymore but my little dog, Horace, has gone missing. Do you know anything about that? Did you mention him to anyone? I have hired a detective and she believes you to be the most likely suspect. Please message back.

Emma's booty call was Edward Foy! The revelation hit me like a slap to my face.

I hadn't seen it. I hadn't seen it at all.

The timings were obvious now that I knew. Emma said he just stopped calling. It would have been about two weeks ago now. She only saw him during the day on weekdays, and he died at the weekend. He hadn't had anything to do with Horace's disappearance though, he couldn't have because he had been dead for a week when Horace was taken.

'How do I access voicemail messages?' I asked, handing the phone back to Barbie so she could fiddle with it. When she handed it back, the most recent one was from Emma, so I pressed play and heard the exact message she left him when I was at her house. It was fairly conclusive.

It closed one line of thought but opened a whole new one. All along I had been trying to work out who the boyfriend could be because he seemed the most likely suspect as the dognapper. Now I had to wipe the board clean and look at the whole thing from a new angle.

First, I was going back to Emma's to confirm and make doubly, trebly sure. When Barbie finished screeching her next set of commands, I said, 'I have to go. I'll leave you to continue torturing those poor people.'

She giggled at me, winked at Sam and jogged back to her position at the front of the group where she picked up the barbell again and yelled, 'Now thrusters! With me!'

I closed the door, leaving her to it. 'Come along, Sam. We need to go back to see Emma.' With my phone at my ear, I waved to Shirley as she buzzed us out and waited for the call to connect. It went to voicemail.

Emma had been taking Horace to the vets, so she was probably still there. That's where I went anyway, guessing right as she was just coming out as I swung the mighty Range Rover into the carpark.

'Wow, this is quite the car,' she said, making her voice loud so it could be heard over the engine rumble. With the window down the engine noise was almost deafening, so I turned the key to let blissful silence return.

Opening the door, I said, 'I think I found Damian.'

'Really?' Emma looked startled. 'Yesterday you had no idea what was going on and why. Now I have my dog back and you've identified the man that took him.'

I shook my head as I opened my phone and pulled up a picture I had of Edward. 'Is this him?' I asked, showing her the screen.

She pursed her lips and looked sad when she nodded. 'Yeah that's him. Do you know why he trashed my house?'

'It wasn't him.' Emma's eyebrows jumped in response. 'He didn't take Horace either.' I sucked in a little air between my teeth as I argued with myself about how to deliver the rest of my news. 'Listen, Emma, I have some information you will not like to hear. He was married. When he was seeing you, he was married, and I think he was seeing other women as well.'

She nodded along as I spoke. 'I guess that's not that much of a surprise. The way he came and went and was never available weekends or evenings kind of gave it away. I should have asked, but I guess I didn't want to know.'

'His name wasn't Damian either. It was Edward. Edward Foy, he lived with a wife and a stepdaughter in Allington.'

'Hold on,' Emma frowned. 'You keep referring to him in the past tense.'

'That's the other bit of news. He died in a climbing accident almost two weeks ago. That's why he stopped calling you and wouldn't answer your calls. It's also why I can be certain he didn't take Horace or break into your house.'

She hit me with a questioning look. 'So, who did?'

Who took Horace was a question I had been trying to answer for four days, but until now, I had no clue and had been looking in completely the wrong place. With Edward Foy as her booty call, I could dismiss the ideas that her boyfriend/booty call was involved. It left me looking in one place, and one place only, but did I actually have any evidence?

The answer was a definite no, but I thought I could create a scenario where the guilty party would accept they had been caught.

I made four phone calls, I got four answers, and I made a plan.

It was time to go to Sarah Foy's house in Allington.

On the way there, I made a fifth phone call, this one to Melissa Chalk. 'Hi Melissa, it's Patricia. I still have Sam with me, do you need him back?'

'Um, no. No, I guess I don't need him for anything. Where are you?' She made it sound as if she was shocked I hadn't returned him already. I found the young man to be perfectly pleasant company though.

'We are on our way to Allington. I have one last stop to make and then I will bring him back. I should have him home for a late lunch. He's proving to be a useful investigator's mate.'

'Right, well, as long as he is no bother.'

'No bother at all.' It felt necessary to be sure Melissa wasn't fretting and with that done I could focus on the task ahead. Not that I had any preparation time left because I had arrived in her street and there were three cars there waiting for me. Five doors opened, DS Mike Atwell getting out of the first, Joshua and Marvin, the two local uniformed bobbies getting out of the squad car parked behind Mike's Volvo and then

Jermaine stepping out of the sleek, shiny, black Bentley Continental as a white man with an impressive grey beard got out of the passenger side.

We met in the street. 'Everyone, this is Sam Chalk.'

Sam held up his hand to wave. 'Hi, everyone. Hi Joshua.' Joshua waved back. That Joshua and Sam knew each other wasn't that much of a surprise. They grew up in the same village, went to the same church each week and had to know all the same people; it was that kind of community.

Jermaine spoke next. 'I have the honour of introducing, Mr Douglas Heiner from Boulder, Colorado. He is a representative of the Sterkiss Climbing Company.' Another very formal introduction. I had to wonder if Mr Heiner now thought all English people talked like Jermaine after spending time stuck in a car with him.

'Thanks,' said Mr Heiner with a nod to Jermaine. 'Just tell me what it is you need me to do.'

'How sure are you?' Mike asked me. He was the senior officer here, so if I had it completely wrong, made a big show, and couldn't make it stick, it would be on his head for allowing it to happen.

I wriggled my lips about as I ran it through my head again. 'About ninety-five percent?' I said it as a question to see how he would react. I believed he and I had some mutual respect, but I had never asked him to put his head in the lion's mouth before. Today I had the opportunity to embarrass him. 'I know why. I even know quite a bit of the how. I just don't know how to prove it. I could work on that and come back if that's what you want. I don't know if I will ever have it though. They hid their tracks really well.'

The gentleman with the impressive beard was itching to say something. I gave him my attention. 'Sorry, Mr Heiner, I should have got to you sooner. You are probably wondering what all this is about.'

'I am a bit, yes.' So I explained as best as I could what it was that we were doing here and what it was that I wanted him to do. I was a little worried that he might not agree to his part, but I felt confident we could get by without him if that was the case. I needn't have worried; as soon as he got that I wanted to bring a killer to justice, he was all over it.

With no reason left to be standing in the street and with curtains beginning to twitch in various windows, I let Joshua and Marvin lead our little procession to Sarah Foy's door.

Joshua rapped on it with enough force to make sure anyone inside would hear. He didn't yell a warning though; this wasn't a raid. A few seconds ticked by before a shadow crossed the light we could see in the frosted glass at the top of the door.

Sarah Foy answered the door with a surprised expression. She hadn't expected to see uniformed police officers. She probably just expected me. 'Whatever is going on?' she asked.

'We need to come inside, Sarah,' I told her, standing with Sam at the back of the group.

Joshua moved forward; a move designed to make her instinctively step back. She did so and the team began moving into her house.

Susie appeared around the door frame of the dining room. 'What's this?' she demanded. 'What's going on?'

It was Mike Atwell that answered her question just as her friend Kara Porter appeared next to her. 'I'm afraid we have uncovered new evidence regarding your husband's death, Mrs Foy.' Sarah put a nervous hand to her chest as she waited to hear what he had to say. 'You were not very truthful with us, Mrs Foy.'

Her eyes bugged right out of her head. 'What?'

I stepped forward, drawing her attention. 'You claimed he was a good husband unlikely to have ever dallied with another woman, always home at the weekends and evenings, but that wasn't true, was it, Sarah? You even told me you would kill him if you ever caught him having an affair after your first husband did exactly that. So, you caught him out, and arranged his death. You even paid a boy to seduce your daughter so she wouldn't be around to see what you were getting up to and couldn't be implicated.'

Sarah Foy was holding her head, a hand either side of her face as her mouth hung open.

DS Atwell took over again, indicating Douglas Heiner. 'This is Professor Douglas Heiner.' Douglas's eyes flared at the invented title. 'He has your husband's quickdraw. He flew in last night from Colorado to prove it had been tampered with. Professor.' Mike handed the floor over to the American.

Suddenly on the spot and feeling every set of eyes on him, Douglas licked his lips and stuttered. 'Um, I.' Then he looked down, looked back up and tried again, producing the quickdraw in a plastic baggy like it was a vital piece of evidence. 'The breaking force the quickdraw has to meet as a minimum is 25 Kilonewtons, which is equivalent to 2.5 metric tons. Furthermore, the sling, which is the part to have failed in your husband's quickdraw is the strongest part of the assembly. If a quickdraw were to fail, it would be one of the carabiners which went first.' He held the quickdraw up for everyone to see as he pointed to it. 'If you look closely

167

here, you can see small marks where one of the carabiners has been gripped in a vice. This would have been necessary for the person to apply enough strain to break the sling. However, even with a mechanical device employed, the quickdraw sling between the two carabiners would still not fail without some additional tampering, which you can see here in the stitching. It is hard to see, in fact, an untrained eye would never see it, but the stitching has very carefully been unpicked along one key edge so that the breaking force required to make this particular quickdraw fail is significantly less. It would require significant testing to determine just what the new figure might be, but one thing is for certain; this quickdraw was tampered with to cause the fall that killed Edward Foy.'

Sarah cried, 'I don't believe this.' Then she repeated it again and again like a mantra. 'I don't believe this. I don't believe this. I'm the one who said it was murder. I'm the one who hired Mrs Fisher to prove it was murder.'

'Yes, a clever ploy on your part, Sarah,' I narrowed my eyes at her. 'You believed there was too little evidence and wanted to be sure no one would ever question the verdict of death by misadventure, so you hired me to delve into every aspect because only then could you be sure that you had gotten away with it.'

Her mouth was hanging open again, the accused woman utterly dumbfounded. Behind her Susie just looked sick, her eyes brimming with tears.

DS Mike Atwell, sniffed in a lungful of air, about to do his job but taking no joy in it. 'Sarah Foy I am arresting you for the crime of murder. Anything you say...'

'No!' screamed Susie, stepping forward. Her cry drowned out Mike's words, forcing him to start again.

'Anything you say…'

'No!' Tears streamed from Susie's eyes. 'No. You're ruining everything. He just fell. Why can't you leave it alone?'

The detective sergeant nodded to Joshua who produced a set of cuffs and moved toward Sarah Foy. Then he tried for a third time. 'Any thing you say may be taken down…'

This time Susie chose to move as well, yelling, 'Stop it!' as she grabbed for Joshua's hands. 'No. Mum didn't do it!'

I felt time freeze for a second. This was it. 'Yes, she did, Susie. I can prove it.' I made sure I sounded haughty and superior, mocking her with my voice.

Her head snapped around to lock her hate-filled eyes on mine. 'No, you can't, you stupid old bat. You've got the whole thing wrong.'

'Susie,' warned Kara.

Susie didn't care for Kara's thoughts though; she was a runaway train with no brakes now. 'My mum didn't kill Eddie. I did.'

Sarah gasped. Kara gasped. Susie sneered at me and no one said anything for three or four seconds until Susie realised it was all over. Then the hate melted away and a single tear fell from her right eye as she bowed her head to look at the carpet and away from the gaze of her mother.

'Why, Susie?' croaked Sarah, her voice breaking as she tried to get the words out.

In the sudden quiet of their hallway, Susie's voice was barely more than a whisper as she confessed. 'I saw him. I saw him kissing that other woman. That artist bitch. She lives opposite Kara. We were bunking off from college and watching TV and he came out of her house and kissed her at the door. Then he kissed her little dog too. His gas van from work was at the kerb so he was there when he was supposed to be working. All those extra hours he was putting in, getting home late all the time. That wasn't overtime. He was sleeping with her. It was obvious they had been having sex. I just couldn't believe it. He looked so happy and he was going to break your heart.' She lifted her head defiantly, tears running down both cheeks now as she looked at her mother. 'I knew you would never forgive him, and you always said you would kill him if he did it, so I arranged an accident. He never suspected a thing.'

Tears were flowing from Sarah's eyes too, but she couldn't stop herself from asking, 'What did you do?'

Susie sniffed and gave a half shrug. 'I asked him to come climbing. I told him how the rocks would be empty at that time of day and we could have the whole face to ourselves. I told him we would get a climb in early and then get home to surprise you with a nice lunch out. I made out it was like a big secret; I needed to make sure he wouldn't mention I was involved. I belayed for him, but when he got to the overhang, I yanked on the rope just as he was reaching for a hold. It was so easy. Once he lost his grip, all I had to do was let go of the rope.'

There was a bit that I hadn't been able to work out. 'How did you get the broken quickdraw into position, Susie?'

She snorted a small laugh, a smile attempting to find its way onto her lips. 'I had to free climb all the way up by myself and put it there.'

Mike Atwell squinted at her. 'But there were no other footprints at the scene and the ground was soft.'

This time it sounded like pride at her cleverness when she said, 'I got out of his side of the car after he did and then stepped in his footprints all the way there and I wore his spare boots. I had to do that free climb in boots five sizes too big. Then I climbed all the way to the top and hiked overland back to Harry's place and got back into bed.' She looked at me again. 'I gave him a pill if you are wondering. That was easy too. I didn't even have to have sex with him. I just had to make sure he remembered me going back to his room and saw me still there when he woke up. Boys are just rubbish. So, you see? It wasn't my mum. You can't arrest her.'

'No,' I replied quietly, my voice still sounding loud in the silence that followed her confession. 'No, we cannot.'

'But he had the extra money from the overtime he was doing,' argued Sarah, unable to let it go even with the evidence now presented.

'He stole it from Emma Maynard,' I told her, filling in another blank as it occurred to me why he had taken her money. 'He might have taken money from other women too.'

'There were other women?' Sarah shrieked.

Detective Sergeant Atwell read Susie her rights as Sarah stood and cried. When they were done, I nodded at Kara. 'Her too.'

Kara's eyes went wide, and she tried to back away, PC Marvin Gaye darting forward to cut off her escape.

Mike looked for me to explain. 'Kara knew all about it, so she was complicit, but she was also involved in taking Emma Maynard's dog. Weren't you, Kara?' Kara didn't answer, perhaps believing keeping quiet rather than admitting everything like Susie might save her. 'Was it because your father absconded with another woman just last Christmas? Did you see an opportunity to even the score for womankind?' She didn't

171

reply to either question, but her eyes betrayed the truth. 'The shed where little Horace the dog has been hidden for the last five days was owned by your father, wasn't it? I called your mother before I came here. It was his allotment. Do you have the key to the padlock on you?'

The panic filling her eyes and desperate desire to run told me they would find the key somewhere in her possession. 'Did you help Susie destroy Emma's work?'

'She deserved it!' snapped Susie, defiant even though she was in cuffs now. 'She's a home-breaking whore.'

I took no pleasure in correcting her. 'She didn't know he was married. She didn't even know his real name.'

It was done. The case, both cases in fact, were solved and closed. Emma had her dog back and they would find the dognapper's phone no doubt when they went through Susie's things. Susie had masterminded the whole thing and might have got away with it. I needed her to confess because I didn't think I could prove she had drugged Harry. It was the only way I could see that she had done it. He gave her the alibi which ensured no one would look at her. It wasn't until Barbie got Edward Foy's extra phone working and I was able to join the dots that I even glimpsed the truth of it. Suddenly there was motive to kill him, but only for Sarah. Sarah would have found out her husband was cheating and plotted to kill him. That was a passionate act though, not the slow, well-planned and meticulously executed murder her daughter devised. It was only when I forced myself to dismiss Sarah that I considered Susie. Yes, she had an alibi, but she also had the skills and knowledge required and just as much motive; to protect her mum from the man who was cheating on her. My ruse to arrest Sarah intended only to cause Susie to confess was a long shot, or might have been, but I was willing to bet that Susie would step forward before she let her mum go down for a crime she hadn't committed.

Sarah wept as they took her daughter away, more police cars arriving because there was evidence to catalogue and rooms to be searched. Douglas Heiner went back out to wait by the cars with Jermaine and Sam, and DS Mike Atwell was outside coordinating everything going on as yet more police arrived. That left me alone with the victim's wife.

'I feel that I should thank you, Mrs Fisher,' she managed between sobs. 'But I don't think I can bring myself to do so. This is even worse than losing Edward. I should have listened to Susie and left it alone. She kept telling me to let it go.' Her head and eyes came up to look at me. 'Why didn't I let it go?' she wailed. She looked utterly wretched.

I didn't answer her. There were no words of comfort I could give. I had done as she asked and proved her husband was murdered. I had to wonder what might have happened if she had let it go and whether Emma Maynard's case would have led me to this point anyway.

A police-appointed grief counsellor arrived to take over which allowed me to drift away. The house was a bustle of activity and the street outside was filled with police cars. Susie and Kara had already been taken away but as I exited the house a familiar figure, that of Chief Inspector Quinn, climbed out of a car. He saw me and made a beeline in my direction.

'Mrs Fisher, in the thick of it again, I see. Congratulations are in order I understand. You caught one that we missed.'

'Hello, Chief Inspector. I think it would have been a hard one to solve had I not been given another case that overlapped with this one.'

'Perhaps you'll have time to explain all that to me later. Right now, I need to make sure everyone is doing their job.' He glanced around at the various uniformed officers going about their business. No one was standing still or looking like they required instruction. 'Oh, I had a call about that Godmother letter. I could do with the original copy if you can bring it by the station or give it to DS Atwell later. My contacts in Scotland Yard put me through to a branch of organised crime specialists who said they have never heard of her.'

I pursed my lips. 'So, you think it might be a hoax?'

'Goodness no. When I said godmother, they instantly put me through to a particular group. They know exactly who she is, they just didn't want to admit it. I believe we should assume she is dangerous and that her threats are serious.' My stomach began to knot. 'I'm afraid the threat against you is probably very real. What I don't know at this time is who she is or why she had taken offense.'

'We can assume it is from my time aboard the Aurelia. That doesn't narrow it down enough though.'

'No, Mrs Fisher. I am sure it does not. I need to deal with this,' he nodded toward the Foys' house. 'Then I think we need to get together and examine your particular case. Please get the original copy of the letter to me as soon as you can.'

'Very good, Chief Inspector. Thank you.'

He nodded and slipped by me, heading toward the house where he was already barking orders by the time I got to the end of the garden path and out into the street.

Mike Atwell, now that CI Quinn was on scene, was essentially unnecessary. He was back at his car and looking to leave, hanging around only to speak to me. 'Two cases solved with one stone, Patricia? Not bad for a day's work.'

I gave him a wry smile. 'Three lives ruined.'

'Not by your hand,' he countered. 'How did you pull all the tiny threads together?'

'Yes, madam,' added Jermaine in his deep bass rumble as he arrived by my side, 'how did you?'

At my car, I paused and turned to face them both. 'I guessed. I made four phone calls on my way here. The first was to Janice Porter, that's Kara Porter's mum to ask about the allotment and the shed. That was a pure hunch. It was the only way I could make the pieces fit. The second to you, Jermaine, to see where you were and if you had been successful with Mr Heiner. The third to you, Mike, to get you here.'

'What about the fourth? asked Mike. 'You said you made four phone calls.'

'Yes. The fourth was to Sarah Foy to ask if her daughter was home. It would have been no good arresting her mum if she wasn't there to see it.'

'A grand bluff,' acknowledged Mike. 'I have never seen or heard anyone else ever doing anything like that.'

I couldn't help but smile. 'That's the advantage of having no idea what I am doing. Or how things ought to be done. I get to just make up the rules as I go.'

Mike Atwell looked at me for a moment, trying to decide if I was joking or not, then burst out laughing. 'Goodness me, Patricia. Being the detective in these parts sure has got a lot more interesting since you turned up.'

I took that as a compliment, opened my car and swung inside, saying, 'Come along, Sam. Let's get you home.'

Unwelcome News

Melissa admitted she was starting to wonder where we had got to when I returned Sam in the middle of the afternoon. He had been with me for nearly six hours, but where she worried he might get bored and start playing up for me, he was overcome with excitement, jabbering away to his mother about all he had seen; the police, and the confession.

We arranged for Melissa to return to my house in a few days so Sam could select a puppy. I thought it quite fitting that he would get to keep one. It also meant at least one of Anna's litter would get to stay locally and we would see it again.

Back home, the first thing I did was call Jerry Brock. I wanted to let him know I had cleared my backlog of cases and would be able to focus on his now. Mostly, I was calling because I promised to start working on it straight away and had not done so because of the days' events.

He was very understanding though also very keen for me to find his daughter, asking several times if I was sure I could now focus on her case. Just as I ended the call and placed the phone on the desk, Jermaine came in bearing a silver tray loaded with afternoon tea. I glanced at the clock just as the big hand swept up to reach exactly four o'clock.

'Will you join me, Jermaine? I eat alone too often.'

I got a smile and a nod. 'Of course, madam.' While he served the tea and set out a small, tiered stand of delicate cakes and finger sandwiches, I looked at what results I had received from sending a blanket message to Helena's social media contacts and Gerard's too. There were a lot of replies, but no one had seen or heard from either of them in a week. I had an itchy feeling in my skull that I didn't like; something telling me this was

177

not going to be a simple case, or even a normal case. It was purely intuitive, and I couldn't explain it.

'Madam?' Jermaine held out the tray of finger sandwiches and poured the tea. Just as I lifted a smoked salmon and cream cheese offering to my lips, Barbie burst through the door.

Bursting through doors wasn't usual for Barbie, nor was the panicked look on her face. Both things got our attention immediately.

'Heavens, Barbie, what is it?' I asked, putting down the sandwich.

She was crossing the room with a hurried pace, her phone in her hands as she fiddled around to select a message to show us. We didn't need to read it though; she was babbling as she handed it over. 'It's from Deepa Bhukari on the Aurelia. I asked her about Mr Schooner and she then asked someone else for an update.'

'He escaped!' I blurted as I read the words on the screen of her phone, the phone itself tumbling from my fingers to bounce on the carpet as a case of the whirlies gripped me.

Jermaine was on his feet and fussing about me. 'Is that right?' he asked; he hadn't had time to read the message.

Barbie collected the phone from the floor and showed him, the two of them talking in urgent, disbelieving tones. I could barely hear them though; my blood was pounding in my ears. Ex Deputy Captain of the Aurelia, Robert Schooner was the man most responsible for my current lifestyle. He had discovered the secret about a massive sapphire and who had stolen it thirty years before and had then instigated a plot to steal it for himself. In so doing, he framed me for a double murder which forced me to uncover my ability to solve a mystery. He didn't come across as the forgiving kind though.

With my head bent low to stop it spinning, I asked, 'Do you think he will come looking for revenge?'

Barbie and Jermaine fell silent, their hushed back and forth stopping abruptly enough to make me question it. 'What? What is it?' I looked up at them.

Barbie glanced at Jermaine. Whatever it was, they didn't want to tell me, but they knew me well enough that such a tactic wouldn't work. Barbie showed me her phone again, keeping hold of it this time so I couldn't drop it on the floor. 'This is a picture of his cell in St Kitts.'

The picture was, in fact, a short video clip that someone had taken with their phone as they panned it around his cell. The rough brick walls were daubed with something to mark them, I worried it might be blood, but whatever it was, was unimportant compared to what had been inscribed. My name appeared over and over and over again. If there had been any doubt about his motivation for escape, it was gone now.

The End

Except it isn't really the end at all. There's a whole load more on the following pages. Scroll down to find out what comes next.

Author's Note

Hello, Dear Reader,

Thank you for reading the first in my new Patricia Fisher Mystery Adventure series.

As I closed this investigation and send it to the editing/proofreading team, it is a frosty morning in early February. I spent all of yesterday redecorating a spare bedroom; despite my desire to do nothing but write, sooner or later it is necessary to tear myself away from the laptop to do something else. Painting, electrics, plumbing, because a new radiator is required, and some electrics because the room only has two sockets and one is behind the radiator all kept me busy until it was time to collect my son from preschool. Then, because I don't own a car (my commute is performed in my slippers) I walked to the next village and piggybacked him one and a half miles home. Usually my wife ferries him around in her car, but she was unavoidably detained elsewhere. It was fun though; the sun was shining, the birds were tweeting, and I had to strip off a layer from the warmth as I smiled my way there and back.

My little house in a country village is right next to a pub, so as we neared my house, and my four year old, Hunter, proclaimed his need for a refreshing cold beverage, I will admit, my arm did not require much twisting. The only issue with a visit to the pub is that it instantly kills my ability to write, but, hey ho.

The next thing on my agenda is to knuckle down and finish the two urban fantasy books I am halfway through and then get back to writing *Solstice Goat*.

Over the next page you can find out about other mystery books I have written and get free books by signing up to receive a newsletter from me.

It's not spam, just my best way of communicating with people who like what I write. In it you will get the best prices for my books, notice of new releases, competitions where you can win books, or get your name in the dedication section of a book, and much, much more.

What's next for Patricia?

Patricia Fisher is trying to settle into village life, but the dead won't let her be. She's a P.I. and used to investigating murder, but her latest case is just … well, it's spooky.

What started as a missing person case goes south fast when a body marked with pagan symbols is found in the woods. It's her client's son-in-law, but the daughter is still out there and a chance encounter with another investigator, none other than famed paranormal investigator Tempest Michaels, sets Patricia on a path of paranormal discovery and starts a race against time to save the missing woman.

The pagan symbols point to a hidden cult and the dread suspicion that they plan to sacrifice her client's daughter at midnight on Orion's solstice.

And that's tomorrow night!

While the police chase false clues, Patricia's super-team follow the breadcrumbs, but they soon discover this case is far bigger than they thought. As they glimpse the truth, and her friends start to go missing, Patricia realises she has come too far to stop now …

Click the cover picture above to get your copy now!

Baking. It can get a guy killed.

When a retired detective superintendent chooses to take a culinary tour of the British Isles, he hopes to find tasty treats and delicious bakes …

… what he finds is a clue to a crime in the ingredients for his pork pie.

His dog, Rex Harrison, an ex-police dog fired for having a bad attitude, cannot understand why the humans are struggling to solve the mystery. He can already smell the answer – it's right before their noses.

He'll pitch in to help his human and the shop owner's teenage daughter as the trio set out to save the shop from closure. Is the rival pork pie shop across the street to blame? Or is there something far more sinister going on?

One thing is for sure, what started out as a bit of fun, is getting deadlier by the hour, and they'd better work out what the dog knows soon or it could be curtains for them all.

All the Books by Steve Higgs

Blue Moon Investigations

Patricia Fisher Cruise Mysteries

Patricia Fisher Mystery Adventures

What Sam Knew

Solstice Goat

Recipe for Murder

A Banshee and a Bookshop

Diamonds, Dinner Jackets, and Death

Frozen Vengeance

Mug Shot

The Godmother

Murder is an Artform

Wonderful Weddings and Deadly Divorces

Dangerous Creatures

Albert Smith Culinary Capers

Pork Pie Pandemonium

Bakewell Tart Bludgeoning

Stilton Slaughter

Bedfordshire Clanger Calamity

Death of a Yorkshire Pudding

Cumberland Sausage Shocker

Arbroath Smokie Slaying

Dundee Cake Dispatch

Felicity Philips Investigates

In Sickness and in Death

Real of False Gods

Untethered magic

Unleashed Magic

Early Shift

187

Damaged but Powerful

Demon Bound

Familiar Territory

The Armour of God

FREE books by Steve Higgs

Get sneak peaks, exclusive giveaways, behind the scenes content, and more. Plus, you'll be notified of Fan Pricing events when they occur and get exclusive offers from other authors because all UF writers are automatically friends.

Not only that, but you'll receive an exclusive FREE story staring Otto and Zachary and two free stories from the author's Blue Moon Investigations series.

Yes, please! Sign me up for lots of FREE stuff and bargains!

Want to follow me and keep up with what I am doing?

Facebook